Don't Be a Stranger

Don't Be a Stranger

John D. Nesbitt

FIVE STAR
A part of Gale, Cengage Learning

Farmington Hills, Mich • San Francisco • New York • Waterville, Maine
Meriden, Conn • Mason, Ohio • Chicago

LIBRARY OF CONGRESS CATALOGING-IN-PUBLICATION DATA

Nesbitt, John D.
Don't be a stranger / John D. Nesbitt. — First edition.
pages ; cm
ISBN 978-1-4328-2929-2 (hardcover) — ISBN 1-4328-2929-7 (hardcover) — ISBN 978-1-4328-2934-6 (ebook) — ISBN 1-4328-2934-3 (ebook)
I. Title. II. Title: Do not be a stranger.
PS3564.E76D66 2015
813'.54—dc23 2014038265

First Edition. First Printing: February 2015
Find us on Facebook– https://www.facebook.com/FiveStarCengage
Visit our website– http://www.gale.cengage.com/fivestar/
Contact Five Star™ Publishing at FiveStar@cengage.com

Printed in the United States of America
1 2 3 4 5 6 7 19 18 17 16 15

for Ric Ramos

ACKNOWLEDGMENTS

The theme song "Don't Be a Stranger" appeared as a poem in *Thorns on the Rose: Western Poetry,* by John D. Nesbitt (Western Trail Blazer, print and e-book, February 2012).

Chapter One

Elwood reined his horse to a stop at the edge of a sandstone bluff. The cream-and-tan-colored formation gave shelter from the breeze, and as Elwood dismounted he felt the reflected warmth of the sun. He held the reins behind him as he stepped through a jumble of waist-high boulders. Around the end of the bluff, a sweep of grassland came into view. The gray hues of winter grass were giving way to the green of this year's growth, and the surface rippled in the afternoon breeze. A quarter of a mile away, a cluster of objects stood out from the even tones of the landscape.

Two men bent over a cow that was stretched out on the ground, and two horses stood back from the animal to hold the ropes tight. Elwood recognized the men right away—Crandall and Beckwith, fellow riders.

Elwood backed away through the boulders and led the horse, a palomino, to stand in the broad sunlight against the bluff. He set his reins and stepped up into the saddle.

He rode the horse into the open and down the gentle slope toward the spot where the two men were working on the cow. Elwood doubted that they were changing a brand. They were way out in the open, and they were not looking around or showing any sign of having something to hide.

The gray horse that Beckwith rode gave an upward motion to its head and made a snuffling sound. Beckwith and Crandall both turned, and Elwood waved to them.

Beckwith stood up and took a drag on a cigarette. Crandall straightened up, stepped back, and wiped a knife blade on his pants.

When Elwood was within thirty yards, he called out. "What have you got?"

Beckwith took another puff, dropped the stub of the cigarette, and twisted the sole of his boot on it. "Old bag had an abscess." He settled his dull black hat on his head as he stepped backward to give Elwood a view.

The cow's side rose and fell. A dark spot spread out on the grass and dirt in front of the animal's belly, and a few blades of grass sparkled red. Elwood caught the whiff of a rotten smell as he swung down from the saddle. He stepped aside so as not to be downwind.

"You lanced it?"

"George stuck it. Damn near a gallon of white stuff came pouring out. Enough to make you sick."

Elwood wrinkled his nose and turned his eyes toward Crandall. The man had put his knife away and had brought out a pouch of chewing tobacco. With his thumb and forefinger he lifted out a wad and stuck it into the side of his mouth. He rubbed his nose with the side of his forefinger and tipped his head back. His gray hat with the upturned brim in front caught the shine of the sun.

"Got to her in time, anyway," Elwood said.

"Oh, yeah." Crandall spit out a gob of juice. "It's easier than when they've got the bloat. You can see exactly where to stick 'em."

Elwood glanced around. "Has she got a calf?"

Beckwith gave a short cough. "Not that we saw."

Elwood's gaze fell on the Crown Butte brand on the cow's hip—a bar with three dots above it, the center dot a little higher than the other two. "Well, a cow's a cow."

"Oh, sure," Beckwith answered. "Always worth savin'. Maybe she'll have a calf next time." His close-set eyes moved side to side as he took out his tobacco sack. He sniffed, rubbed his dark stubble, and began to roll another cigarette.

Elwood raised his head and let his eyes rove across the rangeland. "How's everything else look?"

Beckwith gave a quick nod. "Oh, fine. Just fine."

The cow pulled on the ropes and flailed, raising little clouds of dust.

"Are you done with her?" Elwood asked.

"Oh, yeah. We'll let her up in a minute." Beckwith pulled the drawstring with his teeth, then licked the seam of his cigarette.

Elwood tapped the loose ends of his reins on the back of his hand. "Well, I guess I'll see you back at the ranch."

"Sure." Beckwith popped a match, and as he lit the cigarette he cricked the corner of his mouth and blew out smoke. "We'll be along not far behind you."

Elwood led his horse away a few steps, checked to see that his cinch was tight, and swung aboard. With the sun warm on his back, he decided to take the long way around. He was in no hurry to be the first one back to the ranch.

Elwood slowed his horse to a walk for the last quarter mile into the headquarters of the Crown Butte Ranch. The shadows of late afternoon had begun to stretch from the ridge on his right toward the barn and the boss's house. Across the ranch yard to his left, a thread of smoke rose from the stovepipe of the bunkhouse. As he rode forward, his eyes drifted again to the right, where young elm trees cast shade on the backyard of the ranch house.

Through a gap in the hedge he caught patches of white, yellow, and lavender. The boss's wife and her lady visitor were sitting outside again. Closer now, past the screen of lilac bushes with last spring's clusters gone dry and brown, he heard the women's soft voices. Elwood did not pick up any words or even try to, for what they said was between them. But the melody of women's voices pleased him, and the awareness that one of those voices was new to this country had a charm that he felt free to appreciate.

Inside the barn, he unsaddled the palomino and led it out the back door to the corral. Six horses stood eating at the manger, including the two that Crandall and Beckwith had been riding. Elwood checked to see that the trough had water, then went back into the barn. In the dusky interior he saw the pitchfork leaning against a stanchion, so he picked it up and hung it, tines upward, on the pair of nails where it belonged.

A voice in back of him caught him off guard.

"Hello, El."

As Elwood turned, he recognized the voice and then the person of Rand Sullivan, boss of the Crown Butte Ranch. "Hello, Rand. I didn't see you."

"I just came in. I saw you when you rode through the yard. The others are in the bunkhouse."

"I figured they were."

"So tell me, did you see anything worth noting?"

Elwood gave it a thought. "Not to mention. The only thing out of the ordinary was that Crandall and Beckwith found a cow with an abscess, and they had her stretched out so they could lance it."

"If it's not one thing, it's another. Did she have a calf?"

"They said they didn't see one. I didn't, either."

"There seems to be a little bit of that."

"Abscesses?"

"Cows without calves. Or cows themselves, not as many as you'd think." Sullivan paused. "There just doesn't seem to be the count that there should be."

"That's something like the hunch I had."

The boss's eyes held steady. "I don't think everything's right." Again he paused, as if he was hesitant to say too much. "I think some of it might be going on from the inside."

Elwood picked his words. "A fella has got to be dead sure before he can say anything."

"That's exactly right. For the time being, then, we can take it slow and quiet. Just keep your eyes open. And whenever I send you out on your own, I'd like you to use your own judgment about where to ride and what to look for. Try not to tip your hand, of course."

Elwood nodded. "Sure. I'll do what I can."

Sullivan let the silence hang in the air for a few seconds more. "That's fine," he said. "I'll let you go."

"Good enough." Elwood walked outside, where the late afternoon was slipping into evening. He did not hear voices or see any sign of the women. He looked upward as he heard the wheezing honk of a nighthawk, and as he turned toward the bunkhouse he caught the scent of wood smoke.

He stopped at the door, scraped his feet, and went in. The interior of the bunkhouse had a warm, relaxed atmosphere. A lantern hanging from a rafter cast a glow over the table and cookstove, and the aroma of frying meat drifted in the air. Crandall and Beckwith sat across from one another at the table, while the other two punchers, Foster and Merriman, lounged on their bunks. Otis turned from the cookstove and smiled.

"Grub's on the way," he said.

Beckwith looked up from rolling a cigarette. " 'Lo, El," he said. "Looks like we got back before you did."

"I took it slow." Elwood hung his hat on a peg and rolled up his sleeves.

Crandall was playing solitaire. Without raising his eyes he said, "See anything?"

"Nothing new." Elwood poured water into the basin, cupped his hands, and bent over as he splashed his face. He rubbed his eyes and cheeks, then rinsed them.

Otis whacked a metal spoon on the lip of a pot.

Elwood straightened up as he dried his face. "And how was your day, Otis?"

"Nice and peaceful. Just like yesterday and the day before." He whacked the spoon again. "Beans are ready. So's the meat."

Foster and Merriman rose up from their bunks as Crandall gathered his cards. His mouth opened as he smiled, showing gapped yellow teeth with flecks of tobacco stuck to them. "I wasn't going to win, anyway."

Beckwith blew away a cloud of smoke. "Even if you did win, what would you get?"

"The pleasure of beatin' the Chinaman."

"Big pleasure."

"It's somethin' to do."

Otis set the pot of beans on the plank tabletop. Elwood sat down to the left of Crandall, close to the head of the table. Foster and Merriman took their usual seats on the other side with Beckwith.

Otis set out two tin plates of biscuits, then an oval-shaped platter of fried beef.

"Good grub," said Crandall.

Beckwith took a long last drag on his cigarette and stubbed it out in a sardine can.

Foster spoke up. "See anything, El?"

"Nothing to speak of. How about you boys?"

"Just the regular stuff. Cows are pretty scattered out."

"Seems like."

"Sick ones, too," said Crandall. "There was the one me an' Paul stuck, and then we seen one with lumpjaw after that."

"Did you do anything to that one?"

"Nah, we were on our way back. But we know where she is. We can get a look at her tomorrow."

"Did she have a calf with her?"

"I didn't notice."

Elwood took his turn at lifting meat off the platter. He wondered at a ranch hand, this time of year, not noticing whether a cow had a calf.

Beckwith turned to Foster. "See any snakes?"

"Not yet."

"Time for them to be comin' out."

"Oh, yeah."

Otis sat down at his place at the head of the table, closest to the stove. Elwood took a biscuit and passed the tin plate to his right, then served himself some beans. The talk faded as the men settled into eating.

When the meal was over, the other four hired hands moved down the table a ways as Elwood took his turn at the dishes. He scrubbed one plate after another, setting each one in the pan of rinse water.

At the other end of the table, Crandall was showing a card trick to Foster. The words "Pick a card" were followed by the sound of cards being slapped down on the table and then, "Is this your card?" Crandall gathered the cards and began shuffling them for his next trick.

Elwood slid the last plate into the rinse water, then took out the plates one by one and set them on a towel to dry. He turned toward the stove, where Otis was drying the cast-iron skillet on the warm stove top.

The cook was a lean man with a proportionally large head, a full head of hair, and wide, dark eyes. He had a vacant expression as he stared at the skillet.

Elwood said, "I saw Mrs. Sullivan and her visitor sitting outside."

Otis seemed to come awake. "Oh, yes," he said. "Good weather for it."

"How long do you think she'll visit?"

"No telling. No one's in a hurry, it seems. Weather's just starting to turn nice."

Elwood said, "I've hardly gotten a glimpse of her the couple of times I've seen her."

"Pleasant enough. Neat and clean and well-mannered. What you'd expect in a friend of Mrs. Sullivan's. They went to school together, you know."

"Oh. I don't believe I've caught her name."

"Newton."

"Mrs. Newton," said Elwood.

"That's right."

"What does her husband do?"

Otis held his palm over the skillet, and his eyes were open wide. "As for a living, he's a grain broker."

"I see. Where are they from?"

"Omaha. They're the type that go to concerts and the opera."

Elwood raised his eyebrows. "She must find it rather dull out here."

Otis lifted the skillet from the stove top and set it upside down on the wooden sideboard. "I believe she appreciates the fresh air."

Elwood swished a half dozen forks in the rinse water. The vignette of seeing the women and hearing their voices came back to him, and with it came a pleasant sensation.

Crandall's voice carried from the other end of the table. "Is this your card?"

Rand Sullivan came to breakfast in the bunkhouse, as he often did. He put away the fried potatoes and bacon right along with the boys, and he poured his own coffee. After the meal, as a couple of the punchers rolled cigarettes and lit them, he brought his straight-stem pipe out of his vest pocket. He stuffed the bowl with tobacco and held a lit match over it. The top shreds of tobacco lifted as the boss drew smoke and puffed it out.

"Paul and George, you can work together as you've been doing. Al and Fred, you can check the country over east. You know, we're trying to get an idea of how many we've got as well as where they are."

Foster said, "You bet."

Sullivan took another puff on his pipe. His brown eyes were calm as he turned to Elwood. "You can take a ride up north, El. Same as the other boys. Get an idea of what's out there and where it is." He flicked his finger against the coffee cup. "We'll start working with the horses in another day or two."

"Sure."

Elwood finished his coffee, set the cup by the dishpan, and went outside. The morning was still and clear, cool with a faint touch of humidity. Elwood stood in the dirt yard, taking in the gray sky and the quiet solitude.

The bunkhouse door opened behind him, and he turned to see Al Foster come out.

The young puncher's blond hair and dove-colored hat caught the early-morning light. "Might as well get started," he said.

Elwood smiled. "Best part of the day."

Ten minutes later, having saddled a dark-brown horse from his string, Elwood rode north out of the ranch headquarters. The sun had come up, and long, thick shadows lay across the grass and sagebrush.

Ahead and to the left, movement caught his eye. Two antelope turned to show their white rumps, then turned again. Their white and tan coloring looked gray and almost pink in the growing light.

Elwood rode on, following the contours of the country. When

he was about five miles out, he began a wide loop to the west. He didn't like the feeling of being suspicious and of snooping on his fellow punchers, but he thought he should take a look at the country that Beckwith and Crandall had ridden over the day before. Cattle could go anywhere on open range, but there was something of a natural border out there in the form of a line of buttes. Some of the tricks he had heard of entailed moving cattle and sometimes horses out to the other side.

He had ridden through the butte country many times before, but he always found draws and lesser canyons that looked new to him. There were a thousand hidey-holes for anyone who was inclined to keep out of sight, and in a few places Elwood saw deer tracks leading up into crevices too narrow for a cow or a horse but not for a man on foot.

Elwood paused at the mouth of a small canyon that had a grassy floor with a cow trail worn down the middle of the passage. Up against one side, a clump of chokecherry bushes had begun to leaf out, while along the other side an array of bleached bones lay shining in the sun. He rode into the canyon, following the trail and not thinking about anything in particular, until something out of place caught his eye. He stopped.

In the shadowy side of the small canyon, a black area about a foot and a half in diameter showed where someone had built a fire. Elwood let himself down from the saddle. With the reins in his right hand, he walked to the charred spot. Focusing his eyes in the shadows, he knelt. The fire had burned clean, not leaving any chunks of charcoal. No smell rose from the ashes. Elwood imagined it had been a sagebrush fire, small and discreet and out of view, just the kind someone would use for heating a cinch ring or a running iron. He leaned his face close, and he could feel no warmth. He poked his finger into the center of the ashes. Just as he thought, they were cold.

★ ★ ★ ★ ★

Elwood listened for women's voices as he left the barn, but he didn't hear any. Halfway to the bunkhouse, he let his gaze wander out to the range, and he was surprised to see a stranger about a quarter of a mile away. The man was on foot, trudging along in the trail that led in from the southeast. Elwood waited at the step of the bunkhouse as the man kept walking.

This was wide country for a man to be traveling on foot, Elwood thought, but the stranger hiked right along. He had a knapsack and a walking stick, and his face was shaded by a dusty dark hat. When he was within five yards, Elwood could see his brown eyes, dark mustache, and stubbled beard.

"Evenin'," said Elwood.

"And good evening to you." The man touched his hat, a round-crowned affair with the brim sloping down on all sides, and he took it off with a sweep. His brown hair was plastered with sweat all the way around, and he waved the hat to fan himself.

"Long ways between stopping places," Elwood said.

"I don't mind it. See more this way. As I read once, he who travels fastest goes afoot."

"One way of lookin' at it. I imagine you'd like to wash up, and the good news is that supper's on the way."

The man put on his hat and smiled. "Had to whip the horses to get here on time."

Elwood gave a slight frown in question.

"Shank's ponies." The traveler pointed at his lace-up boots.

"Oh, of course. Well, you did fine. Come on in and meet Otis. He's in charge of the bunkhouse."

Otis invited the man to eat supper and spend the night. "This is a clean outfit," he said. "No greasy spoons or plates, and no bedbugs."

"That's good," said the man. "I've been to places where they made me undress out on the porch, for fear of bedbugs, and even though I didn't have any when I got there, I did when I left. But I assure you I don't have any now."

Otis smiled. "A man should know." He gave the traveler a quick looking over and said, "Go ahead and take off your pack. You can have any one of those empty bunks at the end."

During supper, the man said he was out to see the country. He didn't mind walking, but he usually took a lift when it was offered. Every so often he would stop and work a day or two so he wouldn't be broke. There was no pride in being a vagrant. When Crandall asked him what his name was, he said, "Stanley. D. W. Stanley."

After supper, Crandall went outside with Foster and Merriman to lag pennies. Beckwith had his turn at washing dishes, and his obvious dislike for the chore emanated like an odor. Elwood suggested to Stanley that the two of them go out and watch the penny-pitching.

The sun was slipping behind the butte, and the air was beginning to chill. Elwood went in for a jacket and came back, but the visitor was content to sit with his sleeves rolled up as he smoked his curved-stem pipe. He resisted Crandall's invitations to join the fun, but he was sociable. He told Elwood he had worked as a train crewman and had seen quite a bit of the country from Cleveland to Chicago to Saint Louis to Louisville and back. But one day a steam engine exploded, killing three men, and it had ruined his nerves. He was hoping that when he got through seeing the western part of the country he could go back to work on a steady basis. In the meanwhile he was keeping life simple and taking things as they came.

Elwood said that he and some of the others planned to go to town the following night, as it would be Saturday. They planned to go on horseback as usual, but they could manage the loan of a ranch horse if Stanley would like to wait until then, and they could bring the horse back when they came home.

"Oh, no. That's too much trouble, though I thank you for it. Walking fifteen miles the first thing in the morning is just a warm-up with me. I plan to stay in town for a couple of days, though, so I might see you there, and I'd be glad to have a drink with you."

True to his word, D. W. Stanley was hiking out of the ranch yard at sunup the next morning as Elwood headed for the corral.

A thin man with a thin mustache and a sparse head of hair was playing the piano in the Northern Star Saloon. He was singing an unidentifiable song in a loud nasal voice.

Elwood, Otis, Foster, and Merriman sat around a table. Each man had a glass with about two fingers of whiskey in it, and the bottle stood in the middle of the table. Beckwith and Crandall had come in a little ways behind the other four, and they were standing at the bar.

Otis spoke in a loud voice in order to be heard above the man at the piano. "Not much of a crowd yet."

Elwood nodded.

A line from the song disentangled itself from the rest of the noise.

Through the hills of Virginia he wandered.

The next line was muffled by the man's pronunciation, the banging on the piano, and a loud voice at the next table.

"Let's have drinks. Hey! Give everyone at the table a drink. On me. Jim Farley, the Irishman."

The man speaking was not hard to pick out. He stood by the table with one hand on a cowpuncher's shoulder, and he had the other hand raised to address the five men seated. He had brown hair and a brown mustache, a pale complexion with a pink flush, and merry blue eyes with crow's feet at the corners. He wore a Boss of the Plains hat, rich brown and in new condition, and a corduroy jacket of matching tone. His vest was brown as well, with shiny orange-brown floral embroidery on it. To add to the color, he had a billowy, red silk neckerchief and a clean white shirt. His trousers were clean as well, made of buckskin-colored wool. They covered the tops of a pair of chocolate-brown boots with red stitching and two-inch slanted heels.

He had a slender cigar clamped in his teeth. He took a puff, lifted the cigar away, and said, "You bet. Remember the name. Jim Farley. The Irishman. I'm on my way to Idaho, and I'm goin' to start a town with my own name. You ever get to Idaho, ask for the town of Farley. Then come and see me."

The bartender set five mugs of beer on the table. Farley tossed him a silver dollar and said, "Keep the change."

Movement at Elwood's right caught his attention. He turned and recognized D. W. Stanley, the traveler. "Sit down," he said.

Stanley pulled up a chair as Elwood signaled to the bartender to bring another glass. The man at the piano was still thumping the keys and wailing. Another line floated out.

With never a thought of his mother.

The bartender brought a glass, and Otis poured a drink for their guest.

The gaudy stranger with the red silk neckerchief appeared at the edge of the table. "Hello, boys. Good night to be out, isn't it?" He patted Foster on the shoulder. "I see you've all got a drink, so we'll see about havin' one later." He smiled and showed a good set of teeth. "I'll be back." He raised his hat, which had a crimson liner.

He moved to the next table, made himself known there, and went out the front door. The piano player ended his song, and Elwood took advantage of the lull.

"Spreadin' good will," he said. "His name's Jim Farley, and he wants to name a town after himself in Idaho."

"I know," said Stanley. "I heard him on the way in."

Elwood thought he heard a note of skepticism. "Is that right?"

"Yes. His name isn't Jim Farley, and he's not an Irishman. It's Jude Ostrander, and he's a bank robber. Word is, he's the only one who knows where the loot is from a big job they pulled in Topeka."

Elwood looked at the doorway where the man who called himself Jim Farley had gone out. "I wonder why he's stylin' around here, then. He said he'd be back. Maybe we'll find out."

Stanley took a sip of whiskey. "My guess is that he wants people to think he's someone else."

The noise at the piano picked up again. Stanley sat through one drink, thanked the boys, and took leave. He said he was sleeping at the livery stable and he might see them again.

Chapter Two

Elwood was pouring coffee when Rand Sullivan came to the bunkhouse on Monday morning. Elwood set out another cup and filled it as the boss hung his hat on a peg and sat down. The gray that was beginning to show at Sullivan's temples caught the lantern light. He nodded to Elwood and took out his pipe, then set it aside when Otis set a platter of fried potatoes on the table.

The rest of the men took their seats as Otis laid out the biscuits and two plates of curled, cooked bacon. The men ate without saying much. The boss poured himself more coffee and passed the pot along.

When he was done with breakfast, he loaded his pipe and lit it. After shaking out the match, he spoke through the thinning cloud of smoke. "Boys, I think we'll bring in the rest of the horses today. All those we can find, anyway." He glanced around at Beckwith and Crandall, Foster and Merriman. "The four of you should be able to handle it." He puffed at his pipe. "As for you, El, I've got a different job for you."

Elwood paused with his hands resting on the table.

"My wife wants to show her friend, Mrs. Newton, the old tepee rings on the bluff, so I need you to hitch up the buckboard and be their driver."

"Kids too?"

"Just Quint and Trixie. Mrs. Newton didn't bring any children."

"Of course."

"They'll take along a picnic. I'll leave it to you to keep an eye out for them. Snakes and such. Afternoon storms."

"Sure."

"And I think Mrs. Newton fancies the idea of finding an arrowhead or two."

"I'll be on the lookout."

By the time Elwood had the horses hitched and the wagon drawn up to the ranch house, the sun was beginning to warm the air. He could hear movement and voices inside the house. The Sullivans' yellow cat came into view from the backyard, making its unhurried way to the wooden steps on the front porch, where it settled on the top step and squinted in the sunlight.

The door opened, and Quint came out. Mrs. Sullivan's voice sounded, and the little boy went back in. A moment later, he came out wearing a short-brimmed brown hat and holding a stick as tall as he was. His mother followed, carrying a rectangular wicker basket. Right behind her, the little girl, Trixie, was carrying a folded blanket and a rag doll. Before the door closed, a second lady stepped out.

She had light-brown hair and fair skin, accentuated by the dark-blue dress, jacket, and hat she was wearing. She carried a closed parasol and a brown cloth handbag. She smiled in Elwood's general direction, then looked down and stopped to avoid running into Trixie.

The cat jumped off the step and landed with leisure, stretching and then sitting on its haunches to watch the show. Elwood wrapped the reins on the front rail of the wagon and stepped down to help his passengers.

First he picked up Quint, who was of average size for a six-year-old, and swung him and the stick he carried into the box of the wagon. Next came Trixie, two years older and big enough to be handed up onto the step. Mrs. Sullivan followed. She was wearing a sunbonnet, and her light-blue eye had a pleasant, almost apologetic expression. Elwood took the basket from her and lifted it into the box.

"I put a bed of straw in back for the kids to sit on," he said.

"Oh, thank you. I think I'll sit back there with them." She gave him her left arm, and he helped her up the step. She was not a slender woman, which could be expected of a woman now in her thirties with two children and a household to look after, but she was not a wilting violet. She grabbed the handrail and pulled herself up and into the wagon.

Next came the friend, Mrs. Newton. She met Elwood with a smile and a clear expression on her face. Her eyes were of an uncertain hazel, somewhere between green and brown, and she had pretty lips.

"Would you like to take this?" she said, holding up the handbag.

"Sure." He took the bag, which had clothing that looked like it was for the children, and he set it in the wagon. Turning back to her, he caught a glance at her trim figure as she shifted position and made ready to climb aboard.

She smiled and gave him the parasol, which he hung on the side of the wagon box, and then she gave him her hand. The tan cotton glove was soft to the touch. He held her hand and her elbow as she lifted her foot, a dark buttoned shoe that disappeared in the skirt of her dress. She pulled herself up and shifted so that she did not have her back to him. Looking down, she asked, "Shall I sit on the seat?"

"As you wish," he said, handing her the parasol. "There's room."

Elwood walked around to the other side of the wagon and climbed in. The passengers were settled into their places, so he unwrapped the reins and gave them a shake.

As the wagon rolled out of the ranch yard, Mrs. Newton tugged at her gloves. Then she spoke in a steady, amiable voice. "It's very good of you to be our escort today, Mr. Elwood."

"My pleasure. You can call me El if you'd like."

"Rand says you're a trustworthy man. Capable."

"Then I guess I had better try to live up to that."

She turned to him and smiled. "He says you men lead hazardous lives on horseback."

"Life's a hazard wherever you are. You can be safe in the heart of a city and get blown sky-high by one thing or another. Gas lines, steam engines, anarchists. Out here, you just try not to fall off your horse. And if you do, you try not to land in rocks or cactus."

"I'm sure it's not that simple, Mr. Elwood."

"Everyone calls me El. It really does fit better."

She gave him a humorous frown. "Is that part of your modesty, to go by the smaller half of your name?"

"Hadn't thought of it that way. It's actually short for both my names. Lawrence and Elwood. Lawrence sounds like a wool overcoat of a name, and if I trim it down to L. Elwood—well, you can hear it yourself. Just say El once, and you've got it taken care of."

"That's the way out here, isn't it? Reduce things to their minimum."

Elwood didn't answer.

"I wonder if it comes from living in such big country."

"How so?"

"You have so many things to understate."

"Hadn't thought of that, either."

They rode on for a couple of minutes until she spoke again. "So tell me, Mr. . . . El, what do you think is the biggest danger we might face today?"

"Hail."

"Really?"

"That's right," he said. "Especially this time of the year. Storm can blow up in no time at all, clouds get dark and mean, and you've got hailstones as big as hen eggs."

"Now you're taking it to the other extreme. Poetic exaggeration."

"No, ma'am. Just answering your question."

She looked at the sky. "Do you think we'll get hail today?"

"No tellin'. I hope not."

On top of the bluff, Elwood showed the women and children the circular patterns of stones where Indians had laid out their tepees. He took the lead and went from one point of interest to another, waiting each time for the others to catch up. The stick that Quint had been carrying was Mrs. Sullivan's, for snakes, and she used it as a walking stick as well. She tapped the ground with it and told the children to stay close. Mrs. Newton, carrying her folded parasol, walked along a few yards apart from the others. Though her hat did not have a very broad brim, her face was often out of view as she searched for arrowheads. When she looked up she would squint in the bright sunlight, and when her eyes met Elwood's she would smile.

"I wonder," she said as she came to a stop within a couple of yards of him, "if I have walked right over a hundred arrowheads without knowing it."

"Could be," he said.

"There's a story about Thoreau, the naturalist and writer. He was out showing a fellow around one day, and the man said, 'Where does a person find arrowheads?' Thoreau said, 'Everywhere,' then bent over, picked one up, and gave it to the man."

"It's like what they say about gold. It's where you find it."

Mrs. Newton laid her parasol on her shoulder and spoke without looking at him. "They say that of other things as well."

"For example?"

She hesitated, and though her eyes had a faraway look, they wavered. "Well, love, for one."

"Don't know anything about that. Or gold, either, for that matter."

She gave him an inquisitive look and a faint smile. "And arrowheads?"

"You might be stepping on one."

"Oh, my." She cast her glance downward and stepped backward. "I don't see it. Tell me, do I just not have eyes for them?"

"I don't know."

"Well, what did you see, then?"

"Just your foot." He saw it again, covered by the bottom of her dress.

"Oh. I thought you saw something that looked like an arrowhead."

"No, I just thought there could be one there."

"I see," she said. "You were being philosophical. Or were you? I understand that sometimes men who know the country quite well, who have been here and know the ways, like to have little jokes with newcomers. That's what I am, a tenderfoot, am I not?"

"You might be, that's not my style. Especially with a woman. I was just following your line, the story about the writer fellow."

"Thoreau? I see."

He thought she still seemed skeptical about his motives, so he said, "I don't go in for pranks and tall tales myself. If other fellows want to, that's up to them. But from what I've noticed, a lot of 'em do it to make the newcomer feel like a fool, and at the same time they want to make themselves look smart. The way I see it, though, just about anyone you meet is going to know things you don't, and the other way around. If I were to go back to where you're from—"

"Omaha, we'll say."

"Good enough. So if I were to go there, I wouldn't want you to make me feel like a fool because I don't know how the streetcars run or why the actors do what they do in the opera."

"I should hope not."

"So that's why I'm not fond of lordin' it over the tenderfeet. It's a one-sided game. You find a fella who does that sort of thing—and there's plenty of 'em out here—and you'll find someone who always wants to talk about himself and what he knows, and that's it."

Her voice had a pleasant lilt as she said, "There's your modesty showing again. But you will admit that you know a few things about this country, won't you?"

"I suppose so. A fellow had better know something."

"And it's all so new and different to me, and so . . . fascinating." Her eyes met his. "You can share some of that knowledge without making fun of a poor girl, can't you?"

He shrugged. Maybe she did come for the fresh air and not just to observe the quaintness of the natives. "I don't see why not. Did you have something specific in mind?"

"We'll start with this one thing I've wondered about. Out here you have rabbits and you have hares, correct?"

"The latter being jackrabbits, yes."

"And they're different species, regardless of what they're called. I understand that. Rabbits are born with their eyes closed, and hares with their eyes open."

"That's right."

"Now the rabbits, the cottontails, I notice they run from one place to another, like a clump of brush to a hole in the ground. The theory is that they do that because of all the animals that prey on them—by animals I mean birds as well."

"Good enough."

"But the hare, or the jackrabbit, runs longer distances, out in the open, and when he does, he runs in a zig-zag. Darts off here and there."

"That's correct. I've seen it plenty."

"But why do they do that? Is it for defense, like the cottontail, or is it because of the way their eyes are set in their head?"

"It could be both. I've heard they do it because of their eyesight, but I don't know for sure. Sometimes when they run they stop, and they hold their head up and turn, like they had flat vision."

The woman glanced at Mrs. Sullivan and her children, who had wandered off ahead. "Well," said Mrs. Newton, "if you were to come back in another life, which of the two would you rather be?"

Elwood raised his eyebrows. "I can't say that I'd want to be either of 'em, but if I had to be one, I guess it would be the cottontail. The jackrabbit seems like such a gawky, gangling thing, and the cottontail does get his eyes open in his own good time. How about yourself?"

"Oh, definitely the rabbit." She raised her head and took in a breath as she looked around. "As I said a minute ago, I find this all very fascinating. Things are so spread out, at liberal distances, as they say. One has to take it in differently than the mountains and forests. Isn't that right?"

"Oh, yes. That's one thing you learn, wherever you go in the West. You've got to take the country on its own terms."

"I've heard some people say that the prairies and plains are dull, that there's nothing there, but that's not true, is it?"

"I don't think it is."

"All the little things can be interesting. And the big ones, too, spread out as they are. By the way, can you tell me where Crown Butte is?"

"Yes, I can." He pointed to the southwest. "That's it."

"That tall formation?"

"That's right. Those three points, one on each end and the higher one in the middle, give it its name."

"I see. It does look like a crown, in an abstract sort of way."

"That's how the brand looks, too. With three points."

"Of course. The Sullivans have it burned onto a piece of leather, framed, and hanging in their kitchen." She tipped her head as she gazed in the distance. "And there's a Castle Butte out in this country as well?"

"Yes, there is. About a day's ride to the west, maybe a little less."

"It seems to me I've heard of a Castle Rock as well."

"Oh, yes. And there's not just one. In different parts of the country you'll find places called Castle Rock, Courthouse Rock, Chimney Rock, and other such names. By the way, you're edging kind of close to an anthill there."

"Oh, my. So I am." She moved away from the mound of mineral granules, and he stepped aside to give her room. She pursed her lips and said, "I wouldn't want to be bit by one of them."

"They can raise quite a welt."

She let her eyes meet his. "Then you've been bitten by them?"

"Oh, yes. Even when you think you're careful, they'll sneak up on you."

"And snakes?"

"You can't afford to be careless around them."

Mrs. Newton glanced in the direction of Mrs. Sullivan and the children. "Ellen carries a stick."

"Just as well. Can't be too careful." Elwood looked at the sky. It was clear and blue with no clouds in sight. "We should probably be catching up with them," he said. "We're getting close to noontime."

Mrs. Newton smiled but did not move. "You're very conscientious, just like Rand said."

Elwood shrugged.

"But tell me this, Mr. Elwood, before we move on. You're so capable, and so versed in the ways of the country here. But do you ever make mistakes?"

"I'm afraid so. Much more often than I'd like to admit."

Her eyes met his with a musing kind of expression. "Tell me of one—that is, one that you don't mind admitting."

"I suppose I could, but on one condition."

"And what would that be?"

"That you not call me Mr. Elwood."

"Very well, El." She raised her eyebrows. "And so?"

"I'd have to think for a second. Okay, here's one. You know, you never want to make the mistake of trusting a horse all the way. Sure, there are some that'll never pull a trick on you, but when it comes right down to it, any horse could. You just can't tell. Anyways, there was this one horse, never did anything out of line, and one day we were riding down a canyon, and the trail went one way and another around the rocks, and I must have been daydreaming. Next thing I knew, the horse sidestepped out from under me and dumped me in the rocks. Then he played cat-and-mouse with me all the way back to the ranch. He'd let me catch up to him within fifty yards or so, and then he'd take off in a little gallop. I'll tell you, I was sore after that—not only from the fall, but from hobbling five miles in my boots." He raised his eyebrows. "Is that good enough?"

"Yes, it is. I'm glad to know that even someone like you makes mistakes." After a couple of seconds she said, "How would you categorize your mistake? As being too trusting? Not being skeptical enough?"

"Something like that."

"And that goes for life in general, doesn't it?"

"I suppose so. I always want things to be on the square."

"Doesn't everyone? At least they say so. Oh, I don't mean to say that your idea is common. I can tell you're sincere about it."

"Just the way I am, I guess. But that's probably enough about me anyway. Before we get back to the others, why don't you tell me something about yourself?"

"About me? Well, my name's Josephine. You could call me that if I'm going to call you El."

"I suppose I could. But I meant something else. You see, I told you about a mistake I made. You could tell about one of yours. Nothing serious, of course. Just taking your turn."

She seemed a bit subdued now. She tipped her head and said, "I suppose it's only fair." Her eyes wandered out toward the distant buttes and then came back to him. "This one will do." She moistened her lips and said, "I should have come out here earlier."

"Oh, well," he said. "You're here now. And you seem to be taking advantage of your time. Enjoying the scenery and all."

"That's true. I'm doing what I want. At least in a small way. But as you've already implied, one doesn't always get what one wants." Her eyes flickered away. "And like you've also said, we had better get back to Ellen and the children."

Tobacco smoke hung in a low, level cloud in the bunkhouse. Elwood cleaned and oiled his saddle, keeping an eye out for worn straps, as the other four punchers played a game of Pedro. Crandall and Beckwith, partners, sat across the table from one another, as did Foster and Merriman, the other pair.

Crandall had a continuous line of chatter, calling off every suit that was led and then every card that was laid down. Spades were shovels, clubs were puppy tracks, diamonds were pig eyes, and hearts were bleeders. A king was a cowboy, and the king of diamonds was the one-eyed cowboy. A queen was a whore, and

the queen of spades was the old bitch. Jacks were hooks and sometimes fishhooks, tens were sawbucks, nines were pothooks, and eights were fat ladies. Sevens were walking sticks, sixes were boots, fives were feevers and sometimes nickels, and fours were one-legged aces. The trey was a big butt, the deuce was a duck, and every ace was a bullet.

Otis took a seat near Elwood and drew his tobacco and papers out of his apron pocket. "Find any arrowheads?"

"None today."

"Nice day for it, though."

"Yes, it was. I was afraid things might cloud up, but it stayed clear."

Otis rolled a thin, tight cigarette and lit it. "That it did."

"Any news? It looked like someone dropped off some mail."

"Letter for Al. I think there was an envelope or two for the other house as well. Fella who dropped it off mentioned one little thing that happened in town."

"Oh, what was that?"

Otis glanced at his cigarette. "You remember the showboat that called himself Jim Farley?"

"Of course. Stanley the traveler said he was a bank robber."

"Well, accordin' to the story, he disappeared."

"Just up and vanished?"

"Somethin' like that." Otis took a drag on his cigarette and tipped his ash in a sardine can. "No one saw him for a few days, so they looked in his room at the hotel. Found all of his personal effects there, but no sign of him. No hat or coat. So they figure he left wearin' the same duds he had on that night."

"Huh," said Elwood. "He said he'd be back, but I wasn't surprised when we didn't see him again. But it's hard to imagine him walkin' out into the thin night air and that's it."

"Oh, I imagine he'll show up sooner or later. No tellin' how."

"Maybe in Idaho."

Otis laughed. He took a drag and blew a light stream of smoke. "What's on for tomorrow?"

Crandall's voice came up from the card table. "Puppy tracks."

Elwood came back to the conversation with Otis. "Rand wants me to drop in on Norville. I guess he's not doing well."

Otis shook his head. "Not at all, from what I understand. Hard way to go, livin' alone out on a ranch like that." Otis stared at the floor. "I'll give you a loaf of bread to take along. And I can spare some raisins easy enough."

"And a duck," came Crandall's voice.

A chair leg scraped on the floor, and cards slapped on the table.

"Jack o' diamonds, jack o' diamonds, is a hard card to play."

Otis spoke again. "He probably won't be able to go on roundup."

"We'll see. He might say something about it. For the most part, it's just a neighborly call, drop in and see how he's doin'."

Otis held his cigarette sideways and raised his eyebrows. "If a fella had his choice, he might rather go look for arrowheads."

Elwood shrugged. "One thing about this kind of work. You don't pick your jobs."

The mid-morning sun reflected off the whitewashed ranch house as Elwood rode down the long slope to the west. Nothing stirred in Norville's ranch yard, and no smoke came from the stovepipe. Elwood knew what he hoped not to find, and he made himself look at the corrals. A bay horse with its black mane shining stood broadside to the sun, and a magpie perched on the gatepost.

Except for the footfalls of Elwood's horse, the yard lay in quiet as Elwood rode toward the house. He called out, his voice sounding out of place to him. The bay horse, which had turned to watch, gave a whinny. Elwood's horse, the palomino, answered.

Elwood called again. "Anyone home?"

The door opened, and a thin man appeared in the doorway. The top of his head was pale as he shaded his eyes with his hand. "Mornin'," he said.

"Good mornin', Norville. It's me, Elwood. I ride for Rand Sullivan. He sent me over to see how you're doin'."

"All right, I suppose. Actually, no good."

Elwood swung down, regathered his reins, and untied the cotton bag from the back of his saddle. "Otis the cook sent you this. A loaf of bread, some raisins, and some meat. I hope you don't have a whole beef hangin'."

"Not now. I wouldn't kill one at this point. Don't know how much of it I'd live to eat." Norville lowered his hand as he eyed the sack. "But thanks." He stepped back, and his hand went down to press against his belt, off center and above his right hip.

Elwood stopped at the threshold. "You haven't got appendicitis, have you?"

"Oh, hell, no. I've got the cancer. Slower than appendicitis, but it'll get you all the same, and soon enough. It's eatin' up my guts."

Elwood frowned. "I'm sorry to hear that."

"Nothin' to do about it. But thanks. Come on in." Norville led the way across the small front room and into the kitchen. "You can set it on the table. Thanks."

Elwood took the food out of the bag and set it next to a dirty plate. Then he stood back and put on a half smile. "I'm glad to see you doin' as well as you are."

"Oh, I'm still on my feet. I get around, and I can do my chores. How's Rand? How's everything over your way?"

"Rand's fine. Everything's in good shape. Gettin' ready for

roundup, of course."

"Oh, yeah."

Elwood waited for a comment, and when it didn't come, he said, "Anything I can do for you while I'm here?"

Norville shook his head. "Don't know what it would be." Silence hung for a few seconds until he said, "I'd offer you some coffee, but I haven't made any yet."

"Are you out of it?"

"Oh, no. I've got plenty."

Elwood thought the answer came too quick. Norville's eyes wandered off to the side. The man's hair was thinning on top, but it was still dark. The only gray that showed was on his temples. Elwood recalled what Norville had looked like before, and he didn't think the man could be much past fifty, but he had lost quite a bit of weight and his face had a sunken, haunted appearance.

Elwood gave another try. "If there's anything you need—"

"It was good of Rand to send you over. Tell him thanks. And I'll make good use of this grub. I'm not dyin' that quick."

"You look all right to me."

Now the man's eyes met him. "Sure I do. And thanks for comin' by."

"Glad to be able to." Elwood held out his hand. "We'll see you again."

"You bet."

They shook hands, and Elwood walked to the front door. Outside, he unhitched his horse, tucked the cotton sack in his saddlebag, and took a second to pull the cinch. Norville had stopped at the doorway and was pressing against his belt like before.

"So long," he said. "What did you say your name was?"

"Elwood."

"That's right. I'll remember it next time."

Elwood swung aboard and waved good-bye. Norville raised his hand and waved as well, and his eyes held steady.

A warm, soft wind blew from the west as Elwood drew rein at the top of a rise. He had not seen any signs of humans or human activity for a couple of hours. In a land of grass and sagebrush, rough canyons and sandstone bluffs, he had the illusion that the country rolled on like this forever in all directions. Downslope ahead of him, the grassland lay like a broad, shallow dish. On the other side, a low line of bluffs sat shining in the midday sun.

He rode straight across the dished area, imagining what he looked like from a bird's-eye or a God's-eye view—a hatted rider on a saddled horse moving across the grassland like a bug crawling on a burlap sack.

Up the gentle slope on the other side, he followed the bluff to the left, riding westward until he found a gap in the wall. On a whim, he followed the cow path that led between the sandstone walls. Twenty yards in, the palomino flinched and turned aside, bunching and back stepping to turn around. Elwood got the horse settled down and straightened out, and he gigged it with his spurs to make it go further in.

Around a bulge of stone, the horse stopped again. A dead cow lay on the path.

Elwood dismounted, kept a firm hold on the reins, and walked forward. The cow did not have a strong smell, and it had not been dead long enough to bloat very much. With the toe of his boot, Elwood lifted a hind leg. Stiffness had begun to set in. The cow had a full bag, which meant that it had had a calf. The cow lay on its right side, so the Crown Butte brand was in plain view. A dark red spot behind the left ear, drying in short matted strands of hair, showed where the bullet had entered.

Elwood walked past the dead animal, stepping over the extended legs in the narrow passage, and yanking on the reins to get the horse to follow. Past the carcass, he saw tracks where two horses had gone out ahead. If they had been following a calf, the tracks of the smaller animal were obliterated by the hoofprints of the horses. Elwood knelt. Here was a track, small enough to be made by a calf, pressed into the dirt and surrounded by the marks of horse hooves.

Another thirty yards took him out onto the grassland on the other side of the wall. Again the world seemed to stretch away forever, with no sign of man or his doings. But Elwood knew better. Somewhere out there, an orphan calf had been spirited away, while back in the hole in the wall were the remains of a dirty piece of work.

Chapter Three

Elwood kept from looking at anyone for more than a few seconds as Rand Sullivan lit his after-breakfast pipe and began giving orders for the day.

"Paul and George," he said, "you can ride over east with El today. There's a few more horses to be brought in, and I think at least four or five are hangin' out in that little valley they call Frome Basin. I heard off and on all winter that we had a few head of horses pasturin' there."

Beckwith took a casual drag on his cigarette. "I thought you wanted us workin' over west. There's quite a bit of ground we haven't covered yet."

Sullivan tamped his pipe with the end of his penknife and spoke with his pipe held fast in his teeth. "I know. But we've got to get these horses in and start workin' with 'em."

Beckwith made a slow turn as he tipped his head toward Crandall. "Don't forget your water again."

Crandall smiled, showing smeared bits of tobacco on his teeth. "I'll be fitted out to the last detail."

Sullivan lit another match and drew the flame downward into the bowl of his pipe. "El knows that country better than the rest of you, so just do as he says."

Beckwith covered his mouth and chin as he lifted his cigarette for a drag. His close-set eyes were expressionless as he regarded Elwood and said, "I think El knows all of this country better than any of the rest of us."

Elwood shrugged. "I see something new every day."

Beckwith's eyes held steady on him. Sullivan's eyes did not look up from his pipe as Beckwith said, "What did you see yesterday?"

"I saw a badger den down by Norville's. Right out in the middle of a pasture."

Beckwith glanced at Sullivan and came back to Elwood. "Do you keep track of things like that?"

"Sometimes. If I see a badger hole, even an old one—and this one had fresh dirt packed down in front of it—I try to remember it. They stay around for a long time, and it could be bad luck if your horse stepped in one, especially on a run."

Beckwith blew his smoke upward. "How about Al and Fred? What are they doin' today?"

Sullivan sniffed. "They'll go north. There might be a couple of horses to be rounded up out that way."

"We haven't seen any out west. But like I said, there's plenty of ground out there that we haven't covered yet."

"You know horses," said Sullivan. "But first we'll try the places where I know they've been."

Frome Basin came into view little by little as Elwood and his two fellow riders rode up the long slope to the east. The crest they reached was not very high, but it served as a rim on the prairie. Elwood drew rein to take a look around as the horses had a breather.

The grassland shone in the morning sun, gray and sparse with dark green peeping through. Frome Basin was known for having grass that did not grow as long as in nearby places, but it must have been good-tasting, as horses wintered there every year. As for the shortness, Elwood reflected on what he had heard more than one cowman say: a horse could starve out a cow any day. On first glance today, however, not even horses were grazing in Frome Basin.

Elwood turned to his companions. "We can ride for the high points," he said. "Meet on the other side in about an hour."

Beckwith tipped his head to the left and said, "I'll go this way."

Crandall raised his head so that the upturned brim of his hat caught the sunlight. "I'll go the other way."

"Good enough." Elwood nudged his horse, the dark-brown one from his string, and started off on a slow walk across the middle.

The area had the general form of a basin, as it was called, but it had its gentle dips and rises. Elwood took his time, knowing that an hour was more than enough even for the two riders who were going around the ends.

Less than halfway across, Elwood's horse gave a lurch, pushing back with its front feet and whipping to the left. Elwood pulled the slack on his reins as a full-bodied jackrabbit with a white hind end bolted to the northeast. It ran thirty yards, cut north, ran twenty more, stopped and sat with its ears straight up for a second, and cut to the east. Elwood smiled. It would have been a good sight for Josephine Newton to appreciate.

Elwood waited on the far edge of the valley, looking farther to the east, as Beckwith and Crandall made their way around. Beckwith arrived first, with something like an I-told-you-so air about him. He took his tobacco sack out of his vest pocket, and his close, dark eyes focused on the task of rolling a cigarette.

Crandall came riding up a few minutes later. "Nothin' here," he said. "Looks like this place has been douched out."

Elwood grimaced. Sometimes it seemed as if Crandall went out of his way to say something crude.

Beckwith waved his hand and flicked his ashes. "Shall we go back?"

"We've got plenty of time," said Elwood. "We can go up and

around those bluffs." He pointed to a row of low bluffs, cream-colored on the bottom and tan on top, about a mile to the northeast.

Beckwith wrinkled his nose. "Whatever you say." He lifted his cigarette and took another drag.

"Make some use of our time."

Crandall smiled, showing his crusted teeth. "No hurry," he said. "Unless you got a woman waitin' for you, Paul."

"Puh. Fat chance." Beckwith smoked his cigarette down to a snipe, pinched it out, then twisted the remains and let them fall on the ground. Nodding his head toward the distant buttes, he said, "Any time."

"I've got to go behind the bushes," said Crandall. "You wanta hold my reins?"

Beckwith gave him a sour look.

"Ha-ha. Just tryin' to make a joke. Did you leave your sense of humor back at the bunkhouse?"

"You've got a great future, George. When you get too stove up to punch cows, you can be a comic."

"Maybe a magician. Pull rabbits out of a—"

"Yeah, yeah. We've heard it before."

The three riders covered the distance in less than a quarter of an hour. Elwood led the way around the left end of the buttes and drew up to survey the country even farther to the northeast.

"There's someone over there," said Crandall with a toss of the head. "Looks like they're camped."

Beckwith shrugged, and Crandall spit out a squirt of tobacco juice.

Elwood touched his horse with a spur and set out on a fast walk. Halfway to the camp, he was sure he recognized the light-colored horse. It was pale, not a real white, with a gray mane and tail, and it had been in his string the year before. One of the two others, a sorrel, looked familiar as well.

Movement in the camp drew his eye that way. Two bedrolls lay on the ground, along with a couple of saddles and smaller gear. The bedrolls were still occupied, and one of the men was sitting up and pulling a rifle into his lap. Elwood searched to see if there were any more men, but all he saw was two men and four horses.

Both men rolled out of their blankets and put on their hats and boots. They were both standing, with six-guns on their hips and rifles in their hands, when the three riders came within calling distance.

Elwood could see the speckles on the pale horse, along with the Crown Butte brand. The common-looking sorrel horse, with a narrow blaze and no socks, carried the same brand. Elwood brought his gaze around to the two men and called out. "Good mornin'."

A muttering sound came back.

Beckwith and Crandall had dropped a full length back and had moved out a few yards to either side of Elwood. When the three riders came to a stop, the stranger ahead on Elwood's left raised his voice.

"What do you need?"

Elwood looked from one man to the other, noticed an empty whiskey bottle standing up in back of them, and disregarded it. "We ride for the Crown Butte," he said, "and we're out lookin' for horses. Looks like we found a couple." He motioned with his head toward the animals on picket.

"Strays," said the man on the left. He had a gravelly voice. "Never seen that brand before. Thought we'd turn 'em in, and when the word went out on the wire, we might get a little reward for our good will."

"We're not that far away," said Elwood. "Less than ten miles. And not everyone would call it good will when someone puts a rope on an animal with a brand."

The man made a small motion with his rifle. "If you mean to call us somethin', maybe you should come right out and say it."

"I think I've said things clear enough. We're Crown Butte riders, lookin' for horses with our brand, and we found a couple. The best way to keep things simple is to take your ropes off of 'em. If you wanted to show good will, you could do that right now."

The man's eyes shifted as he took in the three riders. "What if I'm not in the same kind of hurry you are?"

Elwood glanced to either side and saw that Beckwith and Crandall sat relaxed in the saddle and had their hands crossed on their pommels. He thought they could show more support, but he knew he had to forge ahead. He said, "I don't have to be in a hurry. That's how men get hurt. I can take my time and go find a lawman, but I thought I'd give you the chance to do it the easy way."

The man who had been doing the talking looked at his partner. The other man said, "Might as well."

"Go ahead, then. I'll cover you."

The second man frowned.

"Go ahead."

The second man laid his rifle on his bedroll and walked behind his partner toward the horses. The only sound was the tinkle of his spurs until he got close to the pale horse and it snuffled.

The man with the rifle made another motion with it. "How far away is this outfit you say you ride for?"

Elwood said, "I don't like someone pointin' a gun at me."

Beckwith spoke up. "Less than ten miles."

The tip of the rifle lowered. "Never heard of it. Never seen the brand before."

"Well, you have now," said Elwood. He studied the man, in case he needed a description of him later. He was a short, husky man, blue-eyed, with a muddy complexion that might have been freckled at an earlier time. He had brown, reddish hair and a pink nose.

The pale horse, loose now, began to move away from the others with its head lowered in a grazing position. Within a few seconds the other picket rope dropped to the ground, and the sorrel horse moved away on its own.

Elwood turned his horse and spoke over his shoulder at his fellow riders. "We can go now." He whistled and made a clicking sound to split the two loose horses away from the picketed ones. He untied his rope, shook out a loop, and swung it to make it whip in the air. Beckwith and Crandall poked along until Elwood had the horses free. Then they fell in on either side and let him ride out in front as he coiled his rope and put it away. The pale horse and the sorrel knew the other Crown Butte horses, so the group moved together as Elwood hit a lope toward the southwest. He did not look back until they had traveled more than a mile, and by then the strangers' camp was just a cluster of specks moving up and down in the distance.

Elwood was combing out the pale horse's tail when he heard a pleasant voice in back of him.

"Is this one of the horses that was out on the range all winter?"

He turned to see Josephine Newton trimmed out in a light-blue dress, jacket, and short-brimmed hat. Her eyes were bluish-green, a little different from the color Elwood remembered from before. He attributed the change to the color of the outfit she was wearing.

"Yes, it is," he said.

"It doesn't seem to be terribly wild."

"Oh, no. He's all right. He was in my string last year, and he remembers. Takes a little settling down to begin with, and then he'll be fine. I wish they were all like him." Elwood continued pulling the steel comb through the tangles of the horse's tail.

"This land is so expansive," she said. "You go off in some certain direction for several miles, and you come back with horses that have been running wild all winter. Quite impressive to a newcomer, but probably nothing to you."

"Well, it's not quite that easy. You don't find them in the first place you look. And they're not always easy to round up. Sometimes they want to play hard to get."

"Oh, I didn't mean to imply that I thought it was easy. I'm sure it's not something that any old fool can do. What I meant was that you make it seem routine, while to someone like me, this country is like a vast sea. I could no sooner go out and catch a wild horse than I could sail out and spear a huge fish."

"People learn to do both."

"Yes, but it's an entirely different world of experience." She gave him a coy smile and said, "So tell me. Did you make any mistakes today?"

He thought of one, when he assumed he had more backing than he did from Beckwith and Crandall, but he didn't think that was something he should share with someone he didn't know very well. Furthermore, it wasn't his place to tell a story like that, and he doubted that Rand Sullivan spoke very much around women about trouble with other men. "I suppose I did," Elwood said. "But not with horses." He paused, not sure if he should go ahead. Then he said, "I saw some wild roses budding, and I should have cut a sprig to bring back to you."

Her eyes sparkled. "Now aren't you gallant?"

"I don't mean to say anything out of line, but since you expressed an interest in the day-to-day things in this world out here—"

She gave a quick frown to dismiss any semblance of an apology. "Oh, by all means. Now if you don't bring me a sprig, as you call it, you can count yourself remiss."

"I'll take that to heart." He was finished combing the horse's tail, so he put the steel comb in his hip pocket. He moved to the front of the horse, picked up the left foot, and looked at the underside. "So tell me, did you make any mistakes today?" He glanced up and caught her eye.

"I'm sure I made a few, but the one I remember is when I baked a tin of biscuits and let them stay in the oven too long."

He dropped the foot and straightened his back. After looking around and seeing no one within listening distance, he picked up the horse's hind foot and said, "You mentioned something the other day that left me wondering."

"What would that have been?"

"You said you made a mistake in not coming out here sooner. I was wondering in what way you meant it." He dropped the foot and met her eyes again. "I hope I'm not going too far in asking that."

"Not at all." She took a casual glance to either side and said in a voice not very loud, "There comes a time when a woman, or perhaps any person, needs to live her own life."

"I see. So it wasn't as much what you came out here to see as what you—"

"—wanted to get away from."

"Well, that's putting it directly."

She smiled. "I'm learning to speak in short sentences."

"Because we speak in such a plain style here?"

She gave a light laugh. "No, because you never know when someone might walk up."

His hat lifted on one side as he scratched his head. "You make things interesting," he said.

"Actually, if I had taken the trouble to make my sentence longer, I would have said that I also came out here because I did want to see this other way of life, or, as I put it a few minutes ago, this other world of experience. After all, I could have gone to Cape Cod or somewhere like that."

"And learned to spear a fish."

She laughed again and gave a light shrug. "Who knows how much I'll learn out here. But I'm learning *about* things, and it's all quite—worth it."

After a couple of seconds he said, "I got up a jackrabbit when I was out riding today, and I thought of you."

"How nice." After a pause she said, "One thinks of a million things in the course of a day, doesn't he? Have you ever stopped and reflected on how many separate thoughts you had in the span of just a few minutes? It's remarkable."

"I don't believe I've tried it. Maybe I'll remember to do it one of these times."

"I imagine you have time to think," she said. "You ride across this sea of grass, you jump a jackrabbit, you collar a couple of truant horses—I suppose you have intervals during which, if you were a philosopher, you could think about a great many things."

"Depends on the person. Some fellas, their thoughts don't get very high off the ground."

"I've heard that some men turn to the solitary life because they've had some great sadness or some large disappointment."

He ran his hand along the horse's back. "You mean men like prospectors or sheepherders? Those are the solitary ones. The cowpuncher life isn't so solitary, at least not all of the time. But those other types, I suppose some of them go off and live alone so they can nurse their sorrow. The girl who died, the girl who turned 'em down, the girl who ran off with someone else. Yeah, you hear those stories."

"How about you? Do you have any of those sorrows?"

He smiled and shook his head. "No, not really. There have been a couple of times when I had an interest in a girl and things didn't go very far, but I never got dropped on my head. And certainly not anything that would drive me to a hermit's life." He picked up a curry comb where he had left it on the ground and began brushing the horse.

"It strikes me as interesting," she said, "that so many men live lives of bachelorhood. I understand that there's a shortage of women out here, but there must be some element of choice on the men's part."

"I think maybe some of them are suited to the single life, while others fall into it and don't find an easy way to get out. Some do, of course. They meet a girl, settle down, and move into another stage of life. You don't see 'em in the bachelor world anymore, so maybe you don't think of them."

"Then I suppose it's hard to generalize. That's what I need to do, be careful not to draw general conclusions, or laws, as they call them, on the basis of surface appearances."

Elwood shook a thin mat of light-colored hair from the curry comb. "You've got the makin's of a philosopher yourself," he said.

"Just an observer. And not a very expert one at that."

"You don't seem to miss much."

She gave her coy smile again. "Don't be so sure. I might be like a great many other people, and show just what I choose to."

Elwood brought the buckboard to a stop in front of the bunkhouse. The door opened, and Otis came out dressed for a trip to town. He was wearing a short-brimmed, dark-brown hat and a dark-blue wool shirt. On his arm he carried a drab, gray ulster, which he put on before he pulled himself up into the wagon.

"A little chill in the air this morning," he said. "Is there frost?"

"Not that I saw."

"That's the thing about last frost. You don't know if you've seen it yet. First frost, of course, you do."

Otis settled himself on the seat and drew out his tobacco and papers as Elwood got the horses into motion. Wearing his hat and coat, he did not look as lean, and his head did not seem as proportionately large, as when he was dressed in his kitchen duds. He rolled a tight, narrow cigarette as usual, and he lit it as the wagon rattled along the dirt trail. After a couple of minutes he spoke.

"No idea who those fellas were who had the horses tied up yesterday?"

"Nah. I wouldn't be surprised if I never saw 'em again." Elwood paused. "Now that I think of it, I know how I could be surprised. It's like the last frost." A few seconds later he said, "Are you thinkin' we might see 'em in town?"

Otis blew out smoke that streamed away. "You never know. I'd just as soon not."

The sun grew warmer little by little, and by the time they reached town, Otis had taken off his coat.

Elwood pulled the wagon to a stop in front of the general store. He held the reins while Otis let himself down. Otis waited as Elwood set the brake, tied the reins, and climbed down. They went into the store together.

Otis had his list ready and handed it to McDowell, the storekeeper. McDowell was a short, slender man with graying blond hair and large teeth. He wore a white apron that made his teeth look yellow, like a rabbit's.

"I can gather up these things for you," the storekeeper said as he glanced at the list. "Maybe you'd like to take a look around, see if there's anything else."

"Sure," said Otis. He drew out his tobacco sack as the storekeeper walked away. "I think I'll roll myself a pill," he said. "Was there anywhere you wanted to go?"

"Not really," said Elwood. He relaxed and let his eyes wander as Otis went about rolling a cigarette.

An image of dark hair caused Elwood to stop and refocus. A couple of aisles away, a young woman was tending to another customer. She had a light-brown complexion, clear and smooth, and her eyes were dark. She seemed to take notice of Elwood, but then she turned her attention to the customer, a stout woman with a large handbag.

Elwood's gaze drifted back to Otis, who was intent on rolling his thin cigarette. "Is there anything you wanted to look at?"

Otis shook his head. "Nothin' in particular." He put the cigarette in his mouth and struck a match.

"I wouldn't mind lookin' at some leather laces. Always handy if you need to mend somethin'."

"Sure." Otis shook out the match and let it drop on the floor.

Elwood led the way to the end of the aisle and turned. He had lost sight of the young woman.

"I think the leather stuff is over this way," Otis said.

"I believe so." Elwood walked to the third aisle and turned right. Halfway down the aisle he found an assortment of leather laces, thongs, and straps. The smell of oiled and waxed leather hung in the air.

Otis rocked back on his heels and smoked his cigarette as Elwood gave the leather goods a looking over.

"Excuse me." A man in black appeared as if out of nowhere and reached across in front of Elwood. He lifted a pair of straps, narrower than a set of reins and half as long, from a peg and trailed them across Elwood's field of vision.

Elwood moved back, and the man crowded in to finger a pair of saddle strings. The man left the strings on the peg, looked up and down the assortment, and put the first pair of straps back on their peg. He stood still with his hands on his hips, then edged away to the right.

Elwood frowned and took an impression of the man. He wore a dark hat with a curled brim, a black leather vest, a charcoal-colored shirt, and dark trousers tucked into long, black boots that came nearly to his knees. An ivory-handled six-gun stuck out of a black holster.

The man made a quarter turn and reached again for the saddle strings. Elwood caught a profile of his face, clean-shaven with a dark, trimmed mustache and a pointed nose. His beady eyes flickered sideways, and he exhaled short and quick through his nose. He let go of the saddle strings, took hold of the first pair of straps once again, and pulled himself up with a quick breath and turned away from the merchandise. He raised his nose and avoided looking at Elwood as he completed his turn. A silver watch chain flashed, and the ivory-handled six-gun swung around. As the man walked away, the dull shine of his black leather vest matched the shine of his tall boots, and the floorboards creaked.

Otis said in a low voice, "Wonder if he's from around here."

"I don't know if I've seen him before," said Elwood. "He might have been in the Northern Star the other night."

"Are you going to buy some strings?"

Elwood realized he had been gazing in the direction where the disagreeable man had gone. "I'll think about it," he said.

He turned the other way and began to stroll in slow, casual steps. Otis did the same, with his thumbs hooked in his pockets and the last of the thin cigarette stuck in his lips.

They wandered past enamel basins, corrugated washboards, and gray wool blankets. Elwood looked up and around and saw the man in black standing at the counter with the dark-haired young woman facing him. The man said something in a rising tone, and the woman answered in a syllable as she gave him his change.

The woman busied herself with winding the cotton string

back onto the spool. The man lingered a few seconds, taking her in with his eyes. She paid him no attention, and he turned away from the counter. His eyes widened as he saw Elwood and Otis, and his face tensed. His pointed nose lifted, and he could have been looking as far away as Iowa.

McDowell took over the counter as he finished putting together the items on Otis's list. As the storekeeper wrapped the packages, Elwood asked him if he knew the man in the dark outfit.

McDowell broke the string with a tight, practiced motion of his thumbs and fists. "Not at all," he said. "And you?"

"Not sure if I've seen him before."

"Lots of men pass through." McDowell gave an automatic smile. "Couldn't ask for better weather, could we?"

"Not today," said Otis. "But it can change anytime."

McDowell gave him a sincere look and nod. "Isn't that the truth?"

Elwood caught a glance at the dark-haired young woman, who once again was tending to a customer on the floor. It should have been a small matter to learn her name, but as he watched McDowell make another quick snap of the cotton string, Elwood decided he would find out on his own. He stole another look. For all he knew, he might not see her again anyway, but if he did, there would be time enough for him to ask her name.

Elwood and Otis had noon dinner at the café before heading back for the ranch. They each ordered fried chicken, which they hadn't eaten in a while, and for dessert they had peach cobbler.

At the next table sat one of the bartenders from the Northern Star Saloon. He had the pale complexion of a man who worked indoors and slept in the daytime, and from the way he stared at his coffee, he looked as if he was just starting his day. As Elwood and Otis got up to leave, Otis spoke to the man.

"Hello, Ned. What do you know for news?"

Ned blew steam from his cup as he lifted it. "Not much." He took a sip and tightened his eyes. "Maybe one thing is still news if you haven't been to town in a few days."

"Not since Saturday. What is it?"

"You remember that fellow, sort of a hobo, that was here for a few days? Name of Stanley. Had a drink with you-all."

"Sure. He spent the night at the ranch. That's how we knew him. Pleasant enough. Said he liked to walk."

"Well, they found him hanging in the livery stable."

Elwood flinched and said, "The hell. When did that happen?"

"Sunday, Monday, Tuesday morning. They figured he hanged himself. I guess he had troubles with his nerves. That's what he told the stableman."

Elwood shook his head. "He told me about it, too, but I didn't think it was enough to make him do something like that. He told me that when he was done wandering he was going to go back and put his life together again. Go back to work."

Ned let out a tired breath and seemed to exert an effort to raise his eyebrows. "You never know. People say they're goin' to do one thing, and then they do somethin' you'd never expect. I meet all kinds."

"I'm sure you do," said Otis. "Too bad about Stanley, though. Likeable fellow."

Outside on the sidewalk, Elwood let his eyes adjust to the full light of day. He saw the dark stranger from the general store standing in the shadows across the street, so he kept his voice low. "I just can't believe it about Stanley," he said. "He had ideas about what he wanted to do. People who have plans for the future don't hang themselves. Even on a small scale, he said he might see us again. But then again, so did Jim Farley."

Chapter Four

Elwood had his rope in hand and was on his way to the corral when the boss's voice stopped him.

"I say, El. Something's come up."

Elwood paused and turned. Sullivan had stopped as well and was drawing a pair of leather riding gloves across his open palm.

"It's a small thing, but Mrs. Newton would like to go to town."

Elwood gave a questioning look.

"There was a letter for her in the mail that you and Otis brought back yesterday. From her husband, I believe."

An image of the gray canvas bag with its cotton drawstring crossed Elwood's mind. Otis had taken care of it, and Elwood had not paid it much attention.

Sullivan went on. "At any rate, she seems to feel the need to answer it right away, and she'd like to go to the telegraph office."

"I see."

"I can put the other four men to working with their horses. When you get back, they can put the box on the wagon and start stocking it, and you can work with your horses then."

"We roll in three days, don't we?"

"That's right. But don't worry. We'll have things ready. If I could get away I'd take her myself, but I have too many things to tend to."

"It's all right. Whatever needs to be done." After a second's thought, Elwood added, "Does Mrs. Sullivan want to go as well?"

"Not today. She's got plenty of other things to do."

Elwood tapped the coils of his rope against his leg. "Well, I guess I'll hitch up the wagon. If things go well, I'll be back in time to work with the horses in the later part of the day."

Josephine was wearing a gray dress with thin blue stripes, a lightweight jacket of a darker gray, and a dark-blue hat with a rounded crown and a narrow brim. Her eyes had a bluish-gray tone, and she gave Elwood a pleasant smile as he stood waiting to help her into the wagon.

"I want to thank you for taking the trouble to ferry me to town today."

He returned her smile. "It's no trouble. I'm glad to be useful." He gave her his right hand and held out his left to support her elbow. She paused to set her handbag in ahead of her, and then with his help she climbed aboard.

In another minute they were rolling out of the yard. She drew her jacket close and said, "It's a nice day."

"A little cool to begin with. If you get cold, I've got a coat under the seat here."

"Oh, no, thank you. I rather like the cool air. It's bracing."

Out on the open grassland, from time to time they passed little patches of carpet flowers, sometimes white and sometimes yellow, always small.

"It looks as if all these flowers have five petals," she said.

"That's the most common."

"And not much variety in size," she added.

"Not in these, and not at this time of year. Things change as we get into the season."

"And where do the wild roses grow?"

"Here and there. Usually in gullies or low spots where they

catch water. We'll see some."

Less than halfway to town, they came to a draw on his left where the familiar bushes were growing. Elwood brought the horses to a stop.

Josephine gave him a curious look. "Is there something wrong?"

"These are wild roses," he said.

She raised her head to see beyond him. "Oh, they're not very big at all. And they've got five petals as well."

"Yes, they do." He tied the reins and climbed down from the wagon. "Once you cut 'em, the flowers don't last long. Like most wildflowers. But I'll get you a sprig that has buds as well." He took out his pocketknife, found a small branch that had three buds and one open flower, and cut the thorny little stem.

He handed it to her, and she put it in her lap.

"Thank you," she said. "This is rather diminutive—small and delicate."

He climbed into the seat and took the reins. "Well, it's not like a garden rose, with a large bloom and thorns as big as a fingernail."

"It's really quite pretty. Too bad they don't last long, but that's the case with all roses." She took a breath and let out a small sigh. "I could name a dozen poems in which roses mean just that—something short-lived and pretty."

"I don't know a great many poems."

She touched a bud with one finger. "These are something like the desert rose, then, aren't they?"

"I believe they're called a prairie rose."

"I see. They wouldn't be the same thing, would they? I'll try to remember that." She turned the little clipping in her lap and said, as before, "It's really quite pretty." A few seconds later she said, "Ephemeral. That's the word I was looking for."

"And it means—?"

"Lasting a short while. Knowing that about a flower, I believe, adds to one's sense of its beauty. Makes it all the more precious. In this case, the beauty is more subtle than with the roses that come to mind first."

Josephine did not spend much time in the telegraph office. Elwood had just finished watering the horses when she came out. She had a resolved air about her, and she gave Elwood a firm smile as he helped her up into the wagon.

"I suppose we can go back to the ranch now," she said, "unless you have something to do."

"No, I don't. I was just here yesterday, and we took care of everything then." He gave her a quick glance. "Do you think you'll get hungry?"

"Oh, thanks for mentioning it. Ellen sent along some sandwiches. Actually, I made them, but it was her idea." Josephine pointed at her handbag. "Would you like to stop somewhere, or would you just as soon eat as we go? I imagine you have work you'd like to get back to."

He motioned with his head. "Judging from those clouds in the west, we might want to move along. If we get back in time for me to do something, that would be all right as well."

He turned the horses, and the wagon made a half circle. As it straightened out, Josephine put her hands in her lap and straightened her posture.

"Well, it's good to have that task done," she said. "Thank you again for driving me to town."

"Don't mention it. It's worth the company."

"I agree." She lifted her handbag onto her lap and said, "Shall we eat?"

The wind blew cold and damp as the wagon climbed out of a draw and onto a straightaway. Elwood figured they were halfway from town to the ranch, and the clouds were building darker and thicker by the minute.

"Looks like we might get wet," he said. "If you'd like, you can reach back here for my coat and put that around you."

"I'm fine," she said.

"Well, don't be shy. I'm going to make these horses to pick it up a little." He shook the reins and made a loud clicking sound, and the horses broke into a trot.

The rain came a little at a time, in sparse but good-sized drops. A wind seemed for a moment to blow the moisture away, but then the drops came back, at first a scattering and then more steady, until the rainfall became a shower. The smell of damp dust rose from the road, and within a couple of minutes all the earth was damp. Small rivulets were flowing. The water was coming down in sheets, running off of Josephine's hat as she clutched it.

Elwood dipped his head, and water ran off his hat brim in a stream in front of him. The clouds in the west did not have any daylight behind them. "This isn't going to let up very soon," he hollered. "I'm going to try to find a shelter."

She held onto her hat and nodded. Her hair, which had been pinned up, had begun to fall in wet strands.

He turned off the trail to the left, putting the storm at their backs, and held the horses in to keep them from running away. Somewhere out here, he was quite sure, there was an old nester's shack. He had holed up in it a couple of times before, once in a snowstorm and once in a rainstorm like this one.

Small pellets of hail were hitting the ground ahead, jumping up as if they had popped out of the ground. Elwood could feel the stinging of hail on his back.

The mixture of rain and hail gave way to steady hail. The stones were still only pea-sized, but they hurt when they hit, and he knew they could get larger. He let the horses run a little faster.

A quarter of a mile away, the gray form of a shack appeared through the downpour of hail. "Hang on!" he hollered. "It's up ahead."

Josephine was hunched over. She raised her head and nodded.

He pulled the horses to a stop, set the brake, and wrapped the reins. The air was much colder now, because of the hail. He grabbed his coat and jumped down to the ground, where the water had formed puddles. Running around the wagon, he came to a slipping stop at her side of the box.

"Here!" he hollered. He held his arms open, and as she stepped forward, he lifted her clear. He could feel her shivering. He set her on the ground and led her, running, to the shack.

He knew the door was on the leeward side, and he went straight there. He flung the door open and took a quick look around before ushering her in.

The inside was both dusty and damp, as weather leaked between the roof boards on one side of the shack. Hail rattled on the roof like a million gravel stones. Josephine was still shivering, and Elwood moved her to a spot where no water dripped down.

"You're soaked," he said, touching her jacket. "Here, take this off and put mine on."

He had to pull at her cuffs to get the sodden garment off of her. He hung it on a nail and wrapped his coat around her like a cape. Her dress was soaked, and it clung to her body in front as well as in back.

She was not only shivering but shaking, and her eyes were wide open.

His own shirt was soaked, and it wouldn't do either of them any good. He peeled it off, wrung it, and wiped the water off his torso. He hung the shirt on the same nail as her jacket.

"You've got to get warm," he said. He opened the front of the coat he had draped over her, and he pressed his almost-dry body against her cold, wet front. "Hang on to me," he said, "and hold the coat around both of us."

Little by little her shaking diminished as his body heat transferred to her, and her shivers became sporadic. The front of her dress was still wet, but she was no longer cold as ice. Her breathing was smoother now against his shoulder. Her hat had fallen to the floor, and his hand held the back of her head.

"How are you doing?" he asked.

Her head moved, and she drew back from his shoulder to speak. "Better." He lowered his hand to her shoulder, and she looked into his eyes. "Quite a bit better."

The rattling of hail had subsided, and all he could hear outside was the patter and dripping of water. The rest of the world seemed to stretch away into nothing, and there was only the two of them, close together, warmer now, as they both closed their eyes and let their lips meet.

Elwood was working with his third horse of the day, a sorrel with a light-colored mane and tail, when Josephine came out of the ranch house and walked toward him. She was wearing a dark-blue dress with billowy sleeves and an open collar, and she was carrying a parasol.

"Hello," she said. "Hard at work, as always."

"Trying to get caught up." He gave her an appreciative glance. "You're looking chipper. I'm glad the chill didn't stay with you."

"I got into some warm things as soon as we got back, and Ellen fixed me a drink of hot water, brandy, and sugar. I think it did some good."

He looked around, and seeing no one close by, he said, "I'm

glad to see you again. I didn't know if you might . . ."

"Be a stranger?" Her tone was light and cheery. "No, not at all." In a lower voice she said, "I don't have any misgivings about anything that happened."

"Neither do I. As I see it, what happens between a man and a woman is between them—unless there's some kind of trespassing."

"I wouldn't say there was. As I intimated to you as we were leaving town, I had fulfilled a task I needed to take care of. I think I can say, in truth, that I had taken a definite measure to take my destiny into my own hands. From a philosophical point of view, at least, I was free to do as I wished."

He paused in his brushing and said, "I told you you had the makin's of a philosopher."

"Perhaps it was truer yesterday than it was a day or two earlier. Things can change, you know."

"I hope they don't change again right away."

Her eyes met his. "I don't think either of us would go about it that lightly."

"I wouldn't." He felt a strong pull, but he kept himself from moving toward her. Still, he could not let the moment pass him by. He said, "We'll be taking off on roundup in a couple of days."

She pursed her lips in a way that made him want to kiss her. But he kept to himself, and she said, "Well, then, let's not let time pass us by." She took a slow glance around. "Perhaps we can talk more freely later on."

"This evening?"

She nodded. "Among other things, I'd like to know more about the night sky."

"Really?"

"Yes, I'm serious. I understand that you men sleep out under the stars for six weeks at a time. I assume you know something about the sky. By the way, is it true that you always point the wagon tongue north when you make camp at night?"

"I believe that was more the case with cattle drives than it is with roundup crews. In those early times, they were usually traveling north, and a good part of the time they weren't familiar with the country."

"Uncharted seas."

"For them," he said.

"And the wagon tongue was their compass."

"Some of them had compasses, of course, but the wagon tongue was an easy sign, especially when the sky was clouded over. You take these roundup wagons, though. They don't always head north. And the cooks, they usually know where the next camp is going to be, and they can drive right to it."

The sun had dipped behind the buttes, and evening lay on the land. Elwood and Josephine walked at a casual pace along the road that led from the ranch buildings.

"I wouldn't want to seem urgent," he said, "but if there's anything you'd like to ask—or say—we might, well, take this time while we've got it. After all, we do roll with the wagon in a couple of days."

She pursed her lips. "I didn't have a speech in mind, or a set of questions, either. But it seems to me that I might give you a little clearer idea of my circumstances. Does that correspond with what you mean?"

"I think so. A fella likes to know where he stands, but I wouldn't want to have to ask blunt questions."

"That's understandable, to say the least. And I wouldn't want to make a mystery of things. Keep you guessing, as they say."

"Well, that's more than welcome."

She was quiet for a few long seconds as she took a deep breath and exhaled. "I'm not sure exactly where to begin, but

I'll start by saying that for many years I've been married to a cad. Over and over again he has done things that show disregard for the common expectations of a married man. I find the particulars so repugnant that I can't bring myself to repeat them. I hope it suffices to say that his actions have been flagrant and, to me, degrading. When I felt I had reached the limit, I left him. I came here to think things out at a distance, and after a while, as you may have gathered, he wrote me a letter. He said he was going to come for me and take me back. He couldn't let me do this. Well, I had already decided I was going to begin making decisions for myself, so I wired him to tell him not to take the trouble to come here. I asked him to stay where he was and to leave me alone." After a couple of steps she spoke again. "So that was my frame of mind yesterday, and I haven't retrenched in the meanwhile."

"And I imagine you plan to continue doing the same—"

"Choosing my own course, yes."

Elwood took a slow breath. "That can be a tall order sometimes, can't it? From what I understand, it's not all that easy for a woman to separate from a man if he doesn't want her to."

"The legal steps can be very difficult. But there's a vast fund of evidence to draw from, and he knows it. He hasn't been careful." Josephine raised her chin and looked straight ahead. "Then there's the financial aspect as well," she said. "Some men don't hesitate to flatten a woman. Smash her for good." She moistened her lips. "It can be rather ugly, to see a man cut off a woman without a penny and to reduce her, in effect, to the level of a beggar."

Elwood grimaced. "That doesn't seem fair, though I suppose the laws allow it." He took a studied breath. "I wouldn't want to see that happen—that is, to see things be decided that way."

"I'm not afraid of him."

"Well, a worse moment could come. Please excuse me if I'm going too far here, but I wouldn't want to see you buckle under for reasons of money alone."

She smiled in an assuring way. "I don't think it will happen."

"Even so, let me say this. I haven't made much money in my life, but I have set a little aside, and if a lack of money on your part were to make a difference, I would be willing to help you."

She smiled again. "It's very gallant of you to offer, but I don't think I will have to take you up on it. If I wasn't better situated, I wouldn't go as far as I have gone already."

He breathed easy. "That's encouraging. I'm glad to know it. But all the same, we'll remember that I made the offer, and it's still good."

She paused and turned, and he stopped with her. They had walked far enough from the ranch buildings, and the dark had drawn in close enough, that they stood quite by themselves on the broad rangeland. His hands found hers as their eyes met.

"I'm glad we were of the same mind," she said, "in terms of studying the night sky." She glanced upward to her left. "The moon is already up."

"Half-moon," he said. "And the stars are coming out."

"Of course they've been there all along," she said. "As I read once, we need only wait for the 'obscuring daylight' to withdraw."

He raised his eyebrows. "I haven't heard that before."

"Rather unexpected, isn't it? To think of obscuring things in that way."

With no further signal necessary, she closed her eyes and he closed his as they moved toward each other.

As Elwood worked with the horses the next day, he kept an eye out for Josephine. He thought she might sally out for at least a short while in the sunny part of the day, but she kept to the house.

In the afternoon, a rider came and went. Elwood thought he recognized the man as someone from a business in town, but he couldn't quite place him. Rand Sullivan was in the house when the rider arrived. The man went inside and came out a couple of minutes later. After a brief visit in the bunkhouse, he mounted his horse and headed back toward town.

Elwood found a chance to talk to Otis before the rest of the hands came in to clean up. "Any news from town?" he asked.

"Not much. I guess that fella Stanley wasn't as much of a hobo as some people might think. Just thrifty. He had a hundred dollars in cash on him, as well as a train ticket from Cheyenne to Omaha."

"Omaha? I thought he was from farther east."

"He was. They got in touch with his folks back there and sent 'em what little he had."

"A train ticket. I guess he wasn't a hundred percent afraid of steam engines after all."

"It would have been a long walk, even for someone who didn't mind travelin' on foot."

Elwood still hoped Josephine would come out of the house the next morning, but no feminine forms or garments appeared. The chuck wagon, the riders, and the horse herd moved out of the ranch yard shortly after sunrise. Elwood shifted in the saddle a couple of times and still saw no movement near the ranch house.

At noontime, Elwood turned the dark horse into the rope corral, rested his saddle on its forks, and draped the blanket to dry. As he headed toward the chuck wagon, Rand Sullivan hailed him.

"Say, El, have you got a minute?"

Elwood stopped and tipped back his hat. No one else was within hearing distance, and the boss did not look urgent. Elwood dragged the back of his hand across his brow and said, "You bet."

Sullivan stopped a couple of steps away. His glance went to the horses and came back. "I don't know if this is a word to the wise. Maybe just a word."

"Sure. Go ahead."

"Mrs. Newton got a telegram yesterday. You might have seen that fellow Clark when he came out."

"Oh, yeah. Now that you mention it."

"My understanding is that he's coming to visit. Newton, that is. To the ranch."

Elwood felt a jolt in the pit of his stomach. "Is that right? Is he coming for her?"

"I don't know. No one tells me that much. I just know she got a telegram, and that was the import of it."

Elwood stared at the ground, then raised his eyes. "Well, thanks for telling me."

"I thought you might like to know."

Elwood felt as if he had had the wind knocked out of him. He gave a short, defensive laugh. "It's hard to say what I like. And in some ways, I suppose it's none of my business."

"Mine either, except to the extent that it happens on my place." Sullivan twisted his mouth, then relaxed and motioned with his head toward the first gather of cattle. Dust was rising, and the sound of animals lowing and milling carried across the short distance. "At least we've got other things to think about."

"That we do."

In the evening, the Crown Butte Ranch met up with the other two outfits it had thrown in with to make up a roundup crew.

One outfit was the Jaeger and Wye Ranch, and its six hands were the same men Elwood had known for the last couple of years. They were nicknamed the Jigger-Y waddies, and they were easy to get along with.

The other outfit was called the Top Rail, which had changed hands a few times. At the present it was owned by a group of investors, and the hired men came and went from one year to the next. Elwood caught sight of the last two riders of that crew when they came in at sundown.

He thought he recognized the first one, but the man sat back from the fire and his face was in shadow. The second of the two came closer to the fire, walking with a self-assured, almost careless air about him as he carried his plate of grub. Elwood recognized the man first for his short, husky build and then for his brown, reddish hair, muddy complexion, and blue eyes. As the man sat down, the light from the fire gave a shine to his pink nose.

A Jigger-Y waddie at his left asked him a question, and he answered in a gravelly voice. "Yeah. The Top Rail. We just hired on yesterday."

Elwood did not see the two new riders the next morning. As he poured his coffee by the light of the lantern hanging off the wagon, he asked Otis where the men were.

"They're gone already."

"Did they ride out before anyone gave orders?"

"No, they got fired."

"Fired?"

"That's right," said Otis. "They brought whiskey into camp, and you know that doesn't go."

"Huh. I didn't even catch their names."

"Driggs and Haden, as I heard it."

"Who was the one with the pink nose and the rough voice?"

"That was Driggs."

Elwood frowned. "Well, I can't say I'm sorry they're gone. Those were the two who were holding the horses over in Frome Basin that day."

Otis took a drag on his thin cigarette. "The hell. Well, good riddance, I'd say."

"Me, too. And I wondered if I'd see 'em again. Now I still wonder."

Chapter Five

Elwood coiled his rope as the two Jigger-Y waddies let up the last calf to be branded for the day. The smell of dust and burned hair hung in his nostrils, and the bright sun made him squint. He tipped back his hat and dragged his cuff across his forehead. The horse he was riding, the sorrel with the light-colored mane and tail, relaxed beneath him.

Rand Sullivan, who had been keeping tally, reined his horse around and motioned with his head toward the camp. "Looks like we've got visitors," he said.

Three men were riding onto the flat, grassy area where Otis had set the chuck wagon and the bed wagon. Smoke was rising from the fire pit, and the night wrangler was swinging an ax about twenty yards away. The men on horseback came into better view. One wore a light-colored hat, one wore a dark hat, and one wore a cap with a bill.

"I'll see you in camp," said Sullivan. He clicked to his horse, gave it a touch with his spurs, and rode away.

By the time Elwood got the sorrel horse put into the cavvy with the others, half a dozen punchers from the three outfits were sitting on the ground in various positions. Rand Sullivan was standing in conversation with the man in the light-colored hat while the man in the dark hat stood by, paying attention. The man in the cap held the three horses at the edge of the campsite.

Elwood almost stopped in mid-stride. The man in the dark

hat was the unfriendly stranger he had seen in the general store.

Sullivan waved for Elwood to come over, so he did. The man in the light-colored hat, who was older and heavier than the others, gave him a casual glance, while the man in the dark clothes scrutinized him.

"This is El," said Sullivan. "One of my top hands. Been with me the longest. El, this is Mr. Jennings. I'm sorry, I don't remember your first name."

"Tad. But either name is fine. Keep it simple." He put on a smile that vanished right away, and his face looked beefy beneath the wide brim of his cream-colored hat.

"Mr. Jennings is the new owner of the Drumm." Sullivan turned to the man in black. "And this is his right-hand man."

"Josh Armitage." The man's beady eyes settled on Elwood as he held out his hand.

Elwood shook, and as he settled back into his regular posture he said, "I don't think we've seen anything with your brand yet, though I'm familiar with it."

"Oh, no," said Jennings. With something of a liquid sound to his voice. "My place is quite a ways over west. We're on our way there now. You might see something of mine when you come around on your swing back." He tipped his head. "Your boss has told us we should spend the night."

"Of course," said Elwood. "Chuck should be on the way pretty soon. If there's anything else I can do for you—"

"Might be. If you could find a box for me to sit on, I wouldn't mind it. Unless you've got a chair."

"We don't have any of those," said Sullivan. He turned to Elwood. "But I bet you could get Otis to empty out a box for the evening."

"That would be fine," said Jennings. "I just don't care to sit on the ground." He squared his shoulders. He was a good-sized man, and he filled out his brown corduroy coat and tan vest.

By comparison, Armitage in his tall black boots, dark leather vest, curled-brim hat, and pointed nose looked slender.

"How about yourself?" Elwood asked.

"I'll sit on the ground," said Armitage, in a voice none too cheery. "Don't put yourself out for me."

Elwood borrowed a box from Otis and carried it to the far side of the fire pit. Jennings had his head tipped back in a pose of listening, while the man with the duck-billed cap had his chin almost resting on the boss's shoulder.

"Just turn 'em in with the rest of the horses," Jennings said. "They've got night help. Get some food when it's served, and that should be good." He put on a smile as he saw the box. "Oh, thanks." He pulled up his pants legs an inch, laid his hand on the pistol that rode high on his hip, and sat down. He yawned and let out a long breath. "I don't think it'll take me much to go to sleep tonight."

Sullivan spoke up. "I'll go see about some extra ground sheets and blankets so we'll have 'em on hand when you're ready for 'em."

Jennings sat up straight with a hand on each knee. In spite of his clothes and his assured manner, he seemed like something of a stranger to cow country. "We won't need much, will we, Josh?"

Armitage turned down his mouth and shook his head. "Nah."

As the roundup hands took their places to eat supper on the ground, Crandall ended up sitting next to Armitage. Crandall had that air about him as if he was about to show a card trick, but he had a plate of grub in his hands and no deck of cards in sight. "It seems like I might have met you before," he said.

"Could be," said Armitage.

"Maybe in Ogallala?"

"Don't think so."

"Do you play cards?"

"Not much."

"Seems like I might have met you in a card game."

"I couldn't say for sure, but I doubt it."

Crandall's voice raised. "Say, were you in the Northern Star about two weeks ago?"

"I don't believe so."

"I remember what night it was. Paul and I got to town after these other boys, and we were standin' at the bar. I thought you were, too. There was a windbag in there named Jim Farley. Buyin' drinks and tellin' everyone who he was. Maybe you remember him."

Armitage stiffened. "Never heard of him. I wasn't out here yet. I got here just a little ahead of the boss."

Crandall took a couple of bites of stew and chewed as if he was working up a thought. "What kind of a calf crop are you expectin' this year?"

Jennings turned where he sat on the box. "What do you know about it?"

"Oh, nothin'. Just makin' conversation."

"Well, we won't know till we get there." Jennings went back to cleaning his plate.

"I hope you have a good season," Crandall went on. "I don't know how familiar you are with the country out here, but some of us have been around a while, and if there's anything—"

"We'll get along fine," said Armitage. He took a bite, chewed and swallowed, and said, "What's your name?"

"Crandall. George Crandall."

"I'll try to remember that if I meet you again."

"Do you not play cards all that much?"

"Just about never."

Crandall chewed as he spoke. "Even at that, you never know when you'll see someone again."

"Uh-huh."

"Take Elwood here, for example."

Armitage seemed to flinch, but he put on a calm demeanor. "How's that?"

"He met some fellas over in Frome Basin and almost had some cross words with 'em. Then the next thing you know, they ride into the roundup camp here, workin' for the Top Rail. They didn't last long, though."

Armitage didn't say anything.

"Had whiskey in camp."

Armitage moved his eyebrows but still said nothing.

Crandall went on. "Fellas like that, they don't last long in any place."

Armitage sopped his biscuit in the soupy part of his stew. "Get to meet more people that way."

"I suppose. You'd know them if you saw 'em again."

Armitage sniffed, and his trimmed mustache went up and down. "What were their names? Maybe I should be on the lookout for 'em."

Crandall made a long face that showed a hint of mockery. "Didn't catch their names. Elwood could probably tell you, though."

Armitage pointed his sharp nose at Elwood and widened his eyes a little.

Elwood resented being put in a position where he had to talk about men he didn't know, but he saw no alternative. "Driggs and Haden," he said. "That's what I was told. I didn't talk to 'em myself."

Armitage shook his head and gave a disapproving expression. "Never heard of 'em."

"Neither had I."

Crandall's voice came up again. "Elwood's got an agreement with 'em. He don't like them, and they don't like him." With a smile, he said, "What did you say your name was?"

"I didn't." Armitage pointed his fork at Elwood. "You can ask him."

Crandall was still riding the wave of his own humor at noontime the next day. He took a seat on the ground near Elwood and said, "I guess that fella's name was Armitage."

"That's how I understood it."

"Not a very friendly sort. Kind of superior. Seems like he found the right man to work for."

"Could be."

"And then the third one. Followed the boss around like a pet duck. That's what some of the other fellas call him. The duck. Never heard his name."

"Well, they're gone now."

"Yep. That's the way it is. People come and go."

The outfit camped on a creek that evening, so Elwood borrowed a bucket from Otis and took the opportunity to wash a shirt. After washing it and rinsing it, he shook it out and held it up. He was surprised at how transparent it was. He could see the chuck wagon, the lantern pole, and a horse tied to the front wheel.

A voice from behind startled him. "El." It was Rand Sullivan.

Elwood lowered the shirt and turned around.

"Here's a letter that came from the ranch." Sullivan held out an envelope.

Elwood frowned as he took it. "Did Jennings bring this?"

"Oh, no. A rep for the Jigger-Y dropped it off on his way to another roundup farther north. He had a couple of things for their boys as well."

"I see. Well, thanks."

"Not at all."

Elwood studied the envelope before breaking the seal. The

handwriting looked like a woman's, and he had a good idea of whose it might be. His heartbeat picked up, and his mouth was dry. He took out his pocketknife and cut the seal without tearing any of the paper. He unfolded the single sheet of paper from within, and in a glance he saw his name and hers.

Dear El:

By the time you receive this, I will have left the ranch and will have gone back to where I came from. For as much as I thought I was breaking bonds, in the end I saw that this would not be a time of change for me. This does not mean that I did not have the intentions I stated at the time, and I would hope that any intimations made by me would not be seen now as having been insincere at the time. To put it in simpler terms, circumstances have changed, and so my situation has changed as well. I am sorry to disappoint any expectations of continued friendship, and if it is any consolation, I would like to say that any change on my part was not caused by anything said or done on your part. I will remember my visit to this country, as you people call it, along with the things I learned about its ways. I am indebted to your knowledge, and I remain

In friendship,

Josie

Elwood read through the letter a second and a third time. He was not at a loss for information, but he felt as if he was missing something in understanding. As he tried to sort things out, he reasoned with himself that he did not need to know why she went back. He understood that people wrote letters the way they did because they assumed that someone other than the recipient, with or without permission, might read the contents.

He felt a deep disappointment that he did not get to see her again, and he hoped she felt the same. Yet he did not know. He was left to wonder if she preferred to do things this way, to send him a bloodless letter instead of telling him in person. She had learned enough of the ways of this country, as she was pleased to call it, to know which way would be considered better. Maybe she hadn't decided her course of action by the time he left for roundup. On the other hand, maybe she had, and when it came to the crunch, she might have decided to end things the way she did.

As he folded up the letter and put it away, he told himself it didn't matter. She was gone, and he might not ever see her again. He held up the shirt again and looked through it, seeing the chuck wagon, the pole and lantern, the tied-up horse, and then the blaze of the campfire. He couldn't kid himself. Of course it mattered how things ended. If she followed the line of least resistance, it meant that he was not that important after all.

Elwood pushed his gather of eight cattle, mixed stuff, over a grassy ridge and stopped to let the palomino have a breather. The afternoon sun warmed his back through the thin shirt, and the air was still. He should have met up with one of the other two riders, Crandall on his left or the Top Rail puncher on his right, by now. He hoped to see them both pretty soon so they could make the last drive together toward the holding ground.

A faint breeze stirred, carrying with it a thin scent of wood smoke. It came from the north where Crandall should be working the draws. Elwood frowned at the thought of Crandall and a little fire out on the range, and he turned his horse to the left.

He rode for nearly half a mile, crossing the long, low ridges that ran east and west. The smell of smoke came and went. When he crossed the fourth ridge, he saw three horses below and to his left. George Crandall sat on one of the horses, the sorrel he had been riding when he left camp. He was looking down at two men who were sitting on the ground and were almost blocked from Elwood's view by the other two horses. Elwood had a hunch about who they were, but he would see in a minute.

He nudged the palomino down the slope. The casual tone of Crandall's voice carried on the air, but Elwood could not make out the words. No one seemed to notice him as he angled his horse down the hillside. Crandall raised a quart bottle of amber-colored liquid to his lips, tilted his head back, and took a drink. He leaned forward to hand the bottle to someone on the ground, and at that point one of them must have taken notice of Elwood on the horse. Crandall sat up straight and wiped his mouth with the back of his hand. He reined his horse backward about a yard, and the two men who had been sitting stood up.

Elwood recognized the shorter, husky man first. Even at a distance of fifty yards, the man's reddish-brown hair, muddy complexion, and pink nose were identifiable. The name went through Elwood's mind. *Driggs.*

The second man, Haden, moved to the side and stayed behind the horses.

Crandall called out in a loud voice. "Well, hallo, Al-wood."

"Afternoon."

"Come checkin' on me?"

Elwood spoke across the shortening distance. "I thought I smelled smoke, so I came to check on that."

Crandall rubbed his nose. "I don't know. I just happened onto these fellas' camp, and I stopped to say a couple of words. I'd introduce you, but I think you know 'em."

Elwood brought his horse to a stop. He nodded at Driggs and then Haden. Beyond them he saw a small circle of rocks with a thin wisp of smoke rising. He did not see any calves or any signs of an animal having been wrestled to the ground.

Driggs's gravelly voice, familiar now, rose on the air. "Lookin' for somethin'?"

"Like I said, I smelled smoke, so I came to see about it."

"Well, you're out of luck. We're not brandin' any calves for you to report on."

"I wasn't lookin' for anything in particular."

"Sure, I know. But where there's smoke, there's fire. Isn't that right? Take a look around. Satisfy yourself."

"I already did."

Driggs had been holding the whiskey bottle all this time, and he set it on the ground. His voice was rough as he spoke again. "Well, you know as well as I do that this is public domain. A man's got a right to camp where he wants. Has a right to pick up deadfall and burn it."

The thought occurred to Elwood that most men would stay out of the way of a roundup, but he had no argument. "That's right," he said.

"But what?"

"But nothing. That's all I have to say."

"To me, anyway."

Elwood gave him a close look. "Not sure what you mean by that."

"Are you the company stool pigeon? Seems to me you might be."

"Call me what you want."

"I've got a hunch you got us fired from the roundup crew."

"Ah, go on. I didn't even know you had any whiskey."

"Oh, you go on. That was just an excuse. I know damn well you went and told your boss you knew me from before, and that queered the deal for us."

"I did no such a thing. If you got fired, it wasn't through anything I said or did."

"A man who's a snitch is bound to lie as well. I know you've had it in for us since that first day. I told you we were gonna turn those horses in. All we wanted was a little reward, if anyone saw fit to give it."

"We got our horses back, and I was willing to leave it at that. Call it a mistake, if anything."

Elwood noticed that Crandall had backed his horse away a couple of more yards, and he wondered if Driggs had understood that action as some kind of an indication that he could be more forward. Driggs rolled his shoulders and put his thumb on his gun belt, then leaned back, picked up the whiskey bottle, and took a slug.

"You don't like me, do you?" he said.

"I don't have to."

"Well, let me tell you, if I want to have a drink here in my camp, I'm goin' to do it. Whether you like it or not."

Elwood shrugged. "Go ahead. All the same to me."

Driggs held the whiskey bottle by the neck, resting it against his leg, while his other hand hooked onto his gun belt as before. His blue eyes glared as he said, "I doubt that it's *all* the same to you. When it comes right down to it, you just don't like me. But that's all right, because I don't like you."

At the edge of his vision, Elwood saw Crandall make a slight motion as if he was snickering. Elwood focused on Driggs and said, "I don't see where any of that matters."

"And I remember something else you said that day. You said you didn't like someone pointin' a gun at you."

"I don't. And I doubt that very many men do."

"Like this?" Driggs drew his gun and waved it in Elwood's direction. As he did so, he gave a relaxed smile that looked as if the whiskey was beginning to take effect.

"Don't be a fool," said Elwood.

"Don't call a man a fool when he's holding a gun. That's sort of foolish, too, don't you think?"

"If anything happens, there's three men here who have seen

you pull your gun. Even if there are only two of them left, it's not good numbers. You know the old saying. Only two men can keep a secret, and even then, one of them has to be dead."

"I never said I was goin' to pull the trigger. Just pointin' it at you. Because I know you don't like it."

Elwood took a deep breath to try to keep himself steady. "If all you're tryin' to do is needle me, why don't you consider your job done?"

Driggs wrinkled his nose, and the corner of his mouth went up. "Because I'm not done." He put his pistol in its holster. "But if you're any kind of a man, you'll get off your horse and show what you can do with your fists. If you're not, you can just turn around and ride away."

Elwood felt a sinking of the spirits. This was the way Driggs could save face, and he was making Elwood do the same.

A sideways glance showed Crandall with both hands on his saddle horn. Elwood swung down from the palomino, pulled his reins together, and held them up. "George," he said, "would you hold my horse for me?"

Crandall, with a matter-of-fact look on his face, said, "Sure."

Elwood took off his belt and holster, rolled them together, and put them in his saddlebag. He hung his hat on the pommel and turned to face his opponent.

A solid fist hit him on the jaw and sent him stumbling. Driggs hadn't bothered to take off his hat or his gun belt, so he must have expected to end things right away. He came after Elwood, swinging, and landed a punch on his shoulder that knocked him further off balance and sent him to the ground.

Driggs stood back and let him up. The man was going to be sportsmanlike when he felt like it.

Elwood got his fists up, and Driggs came at him, swinging roundhouses like before. Elwood deflected the first two and then caught one on the temple. For a second he lost his bearings, and when he came back to himself he lowered his head and held his forearms up to keep from getting battered. Out of the chaos of punching and shoving and jostling, he saw a chance to punch upward at Driggs's pink nose, and he took it.

Driggs's head went up, and his hat rolled away. He settled into his stance again and came back mauling. Elwood punched through and grazed the man's cheekbone. Driggs regrouped and swung on a wide arc, hitting Elwood in the head behind his right ear. Driggs hooked with the other fist, caught Elwood in the back of the head, and sent him stumbling forward and to one side. Driggs grabbed at his arm, let it slip, and took a hold of the back of his shirt. The cloth gave way with a rip, and Elwood fell on his face in the dirt.

Driggs stood back, breathing hard. The smell of whiskey hung in the air, and Elwood imagined the man had gotten winded sooner than he expected. Driggs's voice sounded even rougher than usual. "Had enough?"

"Just a minute." Elwood pushed himself to his feet, stood up straight, and brushed the dirt off the front of his shirt. Driggs stood with a vacant look on his face, so Elwood, thinking that turnabout was fair play, punched him on the jaw.

Driggs went down and came right back up, his blue eyes wide and staring.

"I didn't start this," Elwood said. "I've had enough if you have."

"Come on." Driggs beckoned with his fist, blinked his eyes, and stepped forward.

Elwood feinted high and drove a fist into the other man's stomach.

Driggs staggered back, letting out a whoosh of whiskey breath, and stood up straight. He blinked twice more and pulled in a long, deep breath.

"I'd say that's enough," Elwood said. "Even if you want to

fight some more, I don't."

Driggs took another long breath, bent over, straightened up, and shook his head. "We can finish this some other day," he said.

"I don't know what for."

"Then you don't know much."

Elwood didn't answer. All they were doing now was competing to see who got in the last word. He walked over to his horse, put on his hat, and took the reins from Crandall. "Thanks," he said.

"Don't mention it."

Elwood swung into the saddle and gave the palomino some loose rein. He had the distinct feeling that Crandall had been hanging back like before and would have let anything happen, but in the end he had nothing to complain about, so he let Crandall have the last word as well.

All the way back to camp, Elwood debated with himself how much he should tell Rand Sullivan. It was his job to tell the boss if he saw anything that looked wrong as far as the boss's interests, which meant cattle, were concerned. But there was also a code among riders that they didn't squeal on each other for small things like loafing on the job or having a drink out on the range. He also knew that Crandall would be on the lookout to see how much Elwood would tell.

So he told Sullivan about having come upon Crandall having a few words with Driggs and Haden.

"Did it seem like they were in cahoots?"

"Didn't seem like it to me. But it might have been a step towards friendship."

"Well, there's not much you can do about that. Birds of a feather will find one another sooner or later."

Chapter Six

Elwood tied the speckled horse to the hitching rail in front of the general store and stepped up onto the board sidewalk. Through the window he saw McDowell the storekeeper, with graying blond hair and white apron, holding a shiny boot at chest level. The heel lay in one hand and the front part of the sole in another, and the storekeeper had an earnest expression on his face as he spoke to a burly man whose dark beard covered his face up to his cheekbones. Elwood found the scene encouraging. The woman might be available to wait on him.

The bell on the door tinkled as he stepped inside. McDowell glanced his way, showed his rabbit teeth in a smile, and went back to tending to his customer. Elwood walked down the center aisle, conscious of the sound of his boot heels on the wooden floor, the jingle of his spurs, and the squeak of the floorboards.

The dark-haired woman appeared at the counter, and the sight of her gave him a glow of pleasure. Her hair was clean and wavy, shoulder length, and her light-brown complexion was clear and smooth as he remembered it. She wore a dark-blue dress with ruffles and a low collar, and she did not wear an apron to hide her figure. As he approached the counter, her dark eyes met his, and she spoke.

"Is there something I can help you find today?"

"A shirt."

She looked at his, then met his eyes again. "A work shirt, or something else?"

"I was thinking of a work shirt. I had one wear out on me." Elwood tipped his head in the direction of the storekeeper and his customer. "I suppose there's lots of fellows, in from roundup, lookin' to replace things that wore out."

"Oh, yes. There have been a few come in."

"Shirt gets worn and thin, and it doesn't take much to put a rip in it."

She nodded as she moved away from her place behind the counter. "Let's see what we have."

He followed her to the second aisle over and went past stacks of denim trousers and overalls. A trace of her perfume mixed with the familiar smell of new clothing. The fabric of her dress made a soft rustle, and her hair swayed. Elwood came back to the present moment as she stopped in front of the shirts.

"This is what we have," she said. Casting another glance at the shirt he wore, she asked, "Do you want something in that same style, or something—"

"I like a shirt with a collar, so I'd prefer that. I don't wear a vest all that much, so something with two pockets would be good."

"Oh." She moved to her left, past the collarless, two- and three-button shirts. "More like these," she said, gesturing with her palm up.

"That's the idea."

"Most of these will have buttons all the way down."

He knew she meant they would be more expensive as well. "That's all right," he said.

Laying her hand on a shirt that was sky-blue, she took the placket between her fingers. "This is a good cotton," she said. "Strong, but not stiff and heavy like canvas."

"That's a nice one. Can we unfold it?"

"Of course." She picked it up, took it by the shoulder, and

shook it out. Her eyes met his, and she said, "What do you think?"

He smiled. "You tell me. Will it look good on me?"

"Oh, of course it will. And it's good enough that you wouldn't have to use it just for work." She held it out for admiration.

"Now you've got me worried."

She gave a light frown as she lowered the shirt. "Why?"

"I'll be afraid to wear it. Not want to ruin it."

She laughed, and her eyes sparkled. "Well, in that case, buy another one. A common work shirt."

"You mean both? Buy two?"

"Why not?" She draped the sky-blue shirt over her forearm, where it made a nice match with the dark blue of her dress. "It's your choice."

He shrugged. "I suppose I could. I just got paid, like everyone else in town. It would be like money in the bank if I didn't wear it very often, wouldn't it?" He shifted from her to the merchandise. "But I'd still like something with some kind of a collar and at least one pocket." He moved to the right, and his eyes settled on a drab shirt of gray linsey-woolsey. "Something like this. Now if it gets ripped or stained, I won't feel bad." He picked it up and let it unfold. "I think it'll work just fine."

"Both of them, then?" She held her arm forward.

"Sure. You convinced me."

"You won't be afraid to wear this one, now, will you?" Her eyes had a playful expression as she smiled.

"Oh, no." He paused. "I'll just be selective as to when I wear it."

"That's the best way." She lingered a second and said, "Anything else?"

"Not today. This was all I had in mind."

He followed her to the counter, where she took her place and began to refold the shirts.

"I appreciate your help," he said.

"Oh, it's a pleasure." Her hands were swift as she set the folded gray shirt to one side and took up the blue one.

"My name's El," he said.

"Like the letter?"

"That's right."

"Like an initial. I've known of men who go by Tee, and that sort of thing."

"It's short for Elwood, which is my last name, and it happens to be the initial of my first name. Either way."

She set the blue shirt on top of the gray one. "Would you like these wrapped?"

"I think so. I'll be carrying them back to the ranch." He waited until she cut a piece of brown wrapping paper from the roll and set it on the counter. "And your name?" he asked. "If I'm not too bold."

Her dark eyes held on him for a second as she said, "Sylvie."

"That's a pretty name. It even has an *l* in it."

She set the shirts on the paper and folded up the first two sides. "So does my last name, as far as that goes." She rotated the bundle a quarter turn. "Lamarre." She folded up the other two sides of paper and had the package wrapped and tied in less than a minute. "Here you are, Mr. Elwood."

He laid a five-dollar gold piece on the counter. "Thank you, Miss Lamarre."

She opened the cash box and picked out the coins for his change.

At that moment, McDowell the storekeeper appeared behind the counter. "Thanks so much," he said.

"And thank you." Elwood smiled at both of them as Sylvie counted his change, and then he tipped his hat at her. He picked up his package and turned away. As his boot heels sounded on the wooden floor, he pictured the two of them, merchant and clerk, watching one customer walk away and waiting for the next one. She was all business when she needed to be. She had given her name as Sylvie but called him Mr. Elwood. Smart girl. She had seen the boss coming.

Music played behind him as Elwood stood at the bar in the Northern Star Saloon. The establishment was filling up as evening set in, and he was glad to have found a place at the rail before things got any more crowded. He finished his first beer and laid the mug on the bar top. Within a few seconds, Ned the bartender appeared.

"Another one?"

"Sure."

The mug came right back, with foam spilling over the sides. Elwood slid a quarter to Ned, who picked a dime out of his apron and set it next to the mug.

Elwood turned to watch the two musicians who were playing. They looked like a typical traveling duo. A man in a brown, high-crowned hat played a mandolin and sang, while a woman with dark-blond hair played a fiddle and sang along. They went through well-known songs such as "Lorena," "Red River Valley," and "Green Grow the Lilacs." Elwood was still lingering on the story line of "Red River Valley" when the pair finished the song about the lilacs. The man in the high-crowned hat spoke in a loud voice.

"Thanks for your applause, friends. We're glad you enjoy some of these songs. They're our favorites, too." He had a bushy mustache, and he pushed it up in a second's pause. "And now, if you don't mind, we'll play a little tune we worked up ourselves. Ready, Betty?"

"You bet." The woman nestled her fiddle in place and put the bow in motion. The man picked at the mandolin and began to sing.

Was in the early springtime
When the grass was showing green,
I met a girl in Hartville
On her way to Silver Springs.

With bright blue eyes that sparkled,
And long soft golden hair,
She told me of her father
And the ranch he had out there.

I told her I was headed
For a job some ways from her,
Out east of Rawhide Mountain,
Punchin' cows for the Single Spur.

Her sky-blue eyes they sparkled
As she tossed her hair and smiled,
Then touched my arm and murmured
In a voice so sweet and mild,

The man's voice lingered, and the woman began to sing. Her lines were plaintive and more drawn out than his.

Darlin', don't be a stranger
When time is on your hands.
You're just one range over
In a large and lonesome land.

It takes a bit of courage
If you're a worthy man,
So don't be a stranger,
Come and see me when you can.

The man came back with his part, and the tempo picked up as before.

I worked those cows on roundup,
Finished up by mid-July,
Then turned my pony westward
To the girl with bright blue eyes.

While crossin' Rawhide Mountain
On the ridges up on high,
I heard the wind a-whisperin'
With a murmur and a sigh.

The night grew dark and lonely,
As I heard the night bird sing
And recalled the voice so tender
Of the girl from Silver Springs.

The woman's voice sounded rich with feeling as she sang again.

Darlin', don't be a stranger
When time is on your hands.
You're just one range over
In a large and lonesome land.

It takes a bit of courage
If you're a worthy man,
So don't be a stranger,
Come and see me when you can.

The man with the mandolin played a few bars and resumed his part, again at a slightly faster pace.

On down the slope of Rawhide,
After riding two days straight,
I found the trail I needed,
And I tied up at her gate.

She seemed surprised to see me,
As a dark cloud crossed her face,
Then her smile came back like sunshine,
And she spoke with easy grace.

She said she'd gotten married,
And was headed farther west.
It'd been so nice to know me,
And she wished me all the best.

She gave her hand in parting,
And I returned the same,
Then stepped into the saddle
And went back the way I came.

As I rode over Rawhide,
Now a stranger to her ways,
Her words came back to haunt me
As my mind was in a haze.

The woman's voice came in again, in a tone that did seem to haunt.

Darlin', don't be a stranger
When time is on your hands.
You're just one range over
In a large and lonesome land.

It takes a bit of courage
If you're a worthy man,
So don't be a stranger,
Come and see me when you can.

The man's voice was strong and clear as his part came back on a lope.

As I ride the lonesome canyons
And the grasslands of this range,
It gives me time to ponder
Those ways that seem so strange.

I ride my horse in twilight
As the mournful night owl sings,
And his voice recalls the soft words
Of the girl from Silver Springs.

I can't forget the sweetness
As her words run through my head,
And I think that at the moment
She had meant what she had said.

Her words, though false they've proven,
Have a calm effect on me,
For they help me see quite clearly
What was never meant to be.

The woman's voice came back in, her voice mournful as ever, as she sang the final chorus.

Darlin', don't be a stranger
When time is on your hands.
You're just one range over
In a large and lonesome land.

It takes a bit of courage
If you're a worthy man,
So don't be a stranger,
Come and see me when you can.

By this point, all conversation in the saloon had stopped, and the crowd was listening to the song. At the end, the two performers gave a slight bow, and the audience applauded. The man took off his hat in salute, then turned it upside down and started it around for collection. He and the woman went about putting their instruments in their cases.

Elwood fell into his own thoughts as the hubbub of conversation resumed. The last song had put him in mind of Josephine. As he recalled, she had even said something to the effect of not being a stranger. Yes, it had been the day after they had been caught in the hailstorm. A cheerful image of her presented itself, Josephine in a felt hat and matching jacket, fair-skinned, smiling, carrying a parasol and standing against a background of rangeland and buttes. He shook his head as the lone, empty feeling poured into him. It did him no good to think of those things.

The upside-down hat came to him. He dropped a two-bit piece on top of the other coins and passed it on. He looked around at the crowd. Close to thirty men, he figured, had come here to pass the evening. Some were seated at tables, some were standing, and some were leaning on the bar. They smoked, chewed, spit, drank, and talked—all in a casual, un-bothered manner as if not a one of them had even been stood up, jilted, or shortchanged. Yet he guessed several of them had, which meant that the sorrow he was nursing was probably pretty common.

Ned the bartender came around and asked if he'd like another beer. Elwood said yes, and the bartender set a mug in front of him.

As Elwood took his change, he said, "So how have things been, Ned?"

"Oh, all right. Just regular. And you?"

"The same." Elwood moved his mug an eighth of a turn and watched the bubbles rise. When one thing got stirred up from the past, it seemed to open the way for something else. "By the way," he said, "do you remember that fellow you told me and Otis about? The traveler they found in the livery stable?" He took a drink.

"Stanley. Sure I remember. What about him?"

"Something I never figured out. They say he had a train ticket to Omaha."

The bartender gave a light shrug and a tip of the head. "That's what I heard."

"Well, I got to know him a little when he stayed over at the ranch. He worked on a train crew himself, but he was from over east of Omaha—Cleveland, Chicago, Saint Louis, Louisville. I wonder why he would have a ticket just to there."

"No tellin'. Maybe he had a pass to ride some of those other trains."

"I just think it's odd he'd go to Omaha. Did he talk to anyone else when he was here in town? Any strangers?"

Ned shook his head. "As far as I know, he kept to himself. You boys were the only ones I saw him say much to, but then again, he didn't come in here much. He did a little work in the stable so he could sleep there, and he paid for his eats. Bought maybe two drinks in here. I thought he'd move on in a day or two, and then he—well, you know how they found him."

"Sure. You're the one who told us. But you know, I've never been convinced he did himself in. Not that I'm doubting you. Just the story. When I talked to him, he had plenty to live for. So it's never made any sense."

"Lots of things don't." Ned pushed himself away from the bar to wait on another customer.

Elwood took a drink and cast another glance around the saloon. As his eyes drifted here and there, they came to rest on a figure that had appeared at the door. He recognized right away the black hat with curled brim, the snug leather vest, and the black stovepipe boots. Armitage lingered long enough to let his beady eyes search the place, and he left.

A pudgy, balding man sat down at the piano and began to plink out a tune.

Da-da-dum da-dum, da-dum-da-dum,

Da-da-dum da-dum-da-dum.

He ran through the same sequence half a dozen times until he began singing in a flat voice.

Oh the country girls have golden curls
When they all come in to town.

Elwood drank up his beer and left the saloon as the man continued to drum on the piano.

The thudding tune stayed with him as he fetched his horse from the stable, saddled up, and made sure his package was secure. To drive the sound from his mind, he recalled the woman with the fiddle and the mournful voice. After a few tries, he had both verses.

Darlin', don't be a stranger
When time is on your hands.
You're just one range over
In a large and lonesome land.

It takes a bit of courage
If you're a worthy man,
So don't be a stranger,
Come and see me when you can.

He sang the chorus of the song several times, and when he left off singing and rode in silence, the coarse melody of the plinking piano came back with the clip-clop of the horse's hooves. So he sang the woman's lines again, then off and on a few times more, as he rode back to the ranch.

Elwood rested his horse in the shadow of a low bluff. The warm, dry wind that had been blowing from the southwest in the late afternoon had calmed to a light breeze, cooler now as evening set in. The horse snuffled, and Elwood patted him on the neck. He had saddled the dark horse for this excursion, and he hadn't given much thought to how much noise it might make.

Ahead of him, a brown hawk skimmed a few yards above a level grassy area about a half mile across. As the land lifted, the hawk did, too, climbing and turning in a wide arc to the right. Off to the left at the same distance, two white spots showed where a pair of antelope grazed on the darkening range.

The sun had made its quick descent behind the buttes, and the breeze was cooler now. The linsey-woolsey shirt was warm enough for this weather, but a cool breeze found any residue of sweat and chilled it.

He touched his spur to the dark horse and rode on in a northwest direction. As dusk gathered, he remembered the three-quarter moon from the night before. There should be good moonlight. He let the horse move at a fast walk. He was in no hurry.

Night had fallen and the moon was up when he saw the dull glow of the line camp. He imagined Beckwith and Crandall sitting at a table playing cards, maybe with a bottle of contraband whiskey. Elwood was prepared not to worry about any liquor. His job was to see if the other two men were where they were supposed to be.

He rode up to the shack and called out. As he dismounted, the door opened and a weak light spilled out.

Beckwith's voice sounded. "Who's there?"

"It's me. Elwood."

"Oh. Well, come on in."

Elwood tied up his horse and went inside. A kerosene lantern hung from a rafter. It did not have a good flame, and the inside of the shack smelled of fumes and smoke. Beckwith was alone, and a hand of solitaire was laid out on the board surface of the table.

Beckwith's close-set eyes settled on Elwood. "What brings you here? Is there something gone wrong?"

"Oh, no. I was just out later than I thought. Got sidetracked a little and thought I'd drop in."

"Do you need something to eat?"

"No, I'm fine. I can wait. I don't want to eat up all your grub."

"It's no trouble. I could fix somethin' up in a few minutes."

"Not at all."

"Well, at least have a seat."

"I can do that." The shack was only about twelve feet by sixteen feet, and Beckwith's chair faced the door, so Elwood set the opposite chair perpendicular to the table and sat down.

Beckwith leaned over and gathered his cards. He sat down, tapped the deck each way to even it up, and set it aside. He was not wearing his hat, and he had a rough appearance with his uncombed hair, narrow eyes, hooked nose, and dark stubble.

"Spend the night?" he said.

"Probably not. Just dropped in to see if you fellas were all right."

"George should be in pretty soon."

Elwood hiked one leg onto another and set his hat on his knee.

Beckwith scratched the side of his nose. "Where you been?"

"Oh, here and there. I was farther south earlier in the day. Then I went up and around and I'm on my way back."

"Seen any rain?"

"Just some dark clouds to the northeast, over Nebraska way.

Anything here?"

"Nothin' at all. Dry as a bone the whole week we been here."

"Uh-huh. Have you had to doctor much?"

Beckwith frowned and shook his head. "Hardly at all. Everything's in good shape here. A couple of calves with stickers in their eyes, and that's about it. You sure you don't want somethin' to eat?"

"No, I'm fine. I'll let my horse rest a few more minutes, and I'll be on my way."

"Good enough." Beckwith took out the makings and began to roll a cigarette. "Everything's all right at the ranch, then."

"Oh, yeah. Grass is startin' to turn dry in most places."

"Here, too. Rand hasn't put on anyone else, has he?"

"Oh, no. I thought he might get someone to pair up with me, but I think he's worried about money."

"I think anyone who's got a ranch has got to worry about money." Beckwith rolled the paper tight and licked the seam. "And they're the ones that have got it all. Take that fat tub Jennings for example. Stinks of money, but tight as a corset."

"I don't know how he is with his money."

Beckwith lit his cigarette. "Just my guess."

The two of them sat in silence as Beckwith smoked. He was almost finished with his cigarette when a soft thudding sound came from outside.

"That must be George. I didn't think he'd be long."

The footfalls of a horse became more audible as they came closer. A minute after they ended, the door of the shack opened and Crandall walked in. He came to a stop less than six feet from where Elwood sat.

His hat with the upturned brim was set back on his forehead, and his eyes had a glaze to them. "Well, hullo," he said, in a show of good humor. "Did you come to check on us, El?"

"I was ridin' by, and Paul insisted that I light and set a while."

"I was gonna put my horse away, but I thought I'd see who was here first. You want me to put yours away, too?"

"Oh, no. I'll be going pretty soon." Elwood put on his hat and stood up. "I should be going now. It's gettin' late."

Crandall drew his head back and seemed to be holding his breath, but the odor of whiskey was on the air. "Don't be in a hurry," he said. "Did you get anything to eat?"

"Paul offered, but I'm not all that hungry."

"You'll be gettin' back pretty late."

Elwood winked. "I might stay in town. Take the long way around. What time is it, Paul?"

Beckwith took out his watch. "Right at ten o'clock."

"Well, then, I'd better move along. I'll see you fellas later."

"You're welcome to stay," said Beckwith.

"Nah, I'd best be going."

"Good enough. Have a safe ride back."

"I'm sure I will. There's a good moon out. Isn't there, George?"

Crandall shook his head as if to wake up. "Oh, yeah."

Outside, Elwood checked his cinch and swung aboard. Beckwith stood in the doorway, and Crandall led his horse to the corral. Elwood clucked to the dark horse and rode away in the moonlight.

Rand Sullivan set down his coffee cup and twisted his mouth in a matter-of-fact way. "As low as the count came out during roundup, especially over that way, you'd think there'd be nothing left to scheme on. But they must have some connection." The boss drummed his fingers on the table. "I'd like to know who's on the other end of it, but you'd have to catch 'em at it, and I don't feel like givin' these two any more rope."

Elwood cast a glance toward Otis, who was keeping his

distance and making plenty of noise as he washed the breakfast dishes.

Sullivan took a sip of coffee and went on. "Al and Fred are doin' all right where they are, so there's no need to change them. So I think I'll do it this way. I'll send you right back out there, and you can take their place. You can stay a week. Don't let yourself be seen very much if you can help it, but get out and around, and see what you can see."

"Go there today?"

"That's right. Take enough provisions for yourself for a week."

"They should have some."

"Better to have too much than not enough. Nothing's going to spoil canned tomatoes, flour, and bacon. It's not like a bushel of eggs."

"All right. Anything else?"

Sullivan's eyes went up to the ceiling and came back. "Nope. Not that I can think of."

Beckwith and Crandall showed no surprise when Elwood showed up with the change in orders. They packed their gear the next morning, and when Elwood asked if there was anything he should be on the lookout for, Beckwith shook his head and said, "No, nothing at all."

For the next week, Elwood did as the boss had said. He rode here and he rode there, and he kept his eyes open. He thought that sooner or later someone might come calling. He imagined the line shack to be something like a salt lick or apple tree that would draw someone like a deer. But in a whole week he saw little of anything—no deer, no snakes, no badgers, and no people. He saw cattle, jackrabbits, and antelope, and even at that, he did not see much.

Chapter Seven

Elwood leaned back in the saddle as the speckled horse took its deliberate steps in the sand and gravel of the slope. The horse listed from one side to another, jabbing and poking its way. Elwood swayed as he leaned. Partway down the draw, he stopped the horse and dismounted on the downhill side, digging his boot heels into the coarse sand to keep from sliding. He walked around in front of the horse and leaned to pick up the object that had caused him to stop. Ten miles from the ranch headquarters, a small, folded piece of white paper lay caught in a tuft of pale green grass.

He picked up the paper, unfolded it, and saw a column of numbers that added up to 19,015. The figures had no context, no words, and no symbols, so he did not know if the numbers represented pounds, bushels, dollars, head of livestock, or something he would never have expected, like pencils. He felt a little silly when he compared the meaningless numbers with what he had hoped for. This far from the ranch, all alone, he could admit to himself that he wished it was a lost letter from Josephine. He tore the paper into small pieces and tossed them into the air to let them flutter away.

He turned the horse around so that he could mount from the uphill side. The horse would not stand still, so he had to pull on the reins to make the animal back up. When the left front foot was planted in a backward step, Elwood stopped the horse and poked his boot in the stirrup. The horse moved its rear end away so that it stood with its hindquarters downhill.

Elwood straightened the horse out, got it into position again, put his foot in the stirrup, grabbed the gray mane with one hand and the saddle horn with the other, and pulled himself up with a quick motion.

Instead of swinging over and landing in the seat, he fell backwards. His toe went under the horse with the stirrup, the saddle and blanket turned, and the whole outfit hung under the belly of the horse as Elwood hit the ground. He landed on his butt, turned, leaned on his elbow, and pulled his foot free of the stirrup as the horse spooked, jumping and sliding away from him with a snort and a wheeze. The reins pulled out of Elwood's hands, and the horse bolted away, grunting as it kicked up its hind feet and tried to shake away the saddle.

Elwood took only a couple of seconds to get to his feet and gather his senses. The pale horse had come to a stop at the bottom of the draw. The saddle hung upside down, attached to the horse by the back cinch. The outfit was twisted to one side, with the swells touching the ground and the blanket spilling out.

Digging his boot heels into the sand as before, Elwood made his way down the slope. At the bottom he took soft, slow steps and spoke to the pale horse. "Whoa, boy. Easy. Nothin' to worry about." The horse gave him a wary eye as he moved closer, then laid one hand on the reins and patted the horse's neck with the other.

Still holding the reins, he crossed in front of the horse and reached back to unbuckle the rear cinch. Looking down, he saw that the front cinch was still attached by the latigo on the rider's side. It had given way on the off side.

With the saddle free and lying on the ground, Elwood led the horse aside and back around so he could study the place where the cinch had broken. This was the type of thing he kept an eye out for, so he wanted to know how it happened. He crouched, took the loose end of the cinch in his hand, and turned it. He saw that the billet, or double strap, that went through the D-ring on the off side had separated at the fold where it pulled on the metal. He couldn't remember having seen that kind of a break before. If something wore out, it was more likely to be the latigo, the long strap that wrapped two or three times from the D-ring to the cinch ring on the near side when a rider saddled a horse and pulled the cinch tight.

Still in a crouch and holding the reins, he took the broken billet in both hands. *Curious,* he thought. He held the two halves of the strap apart so he could see how it had worn and broken on the D-ring. *Curious.* Only the top of the fold was broken. The underside was cut clean, not worn and darkened as it would be if it had worn against the brass ring for a long period of time. He held the pieces together, and he saw that the cut was new, made by a narrower edge than that of the D-ring. It looked as if someone had cut the inside of the fold more than halfway through and had left it to break the rest of the way on its own.

Elwood let out a long, low breath. A break like that could happen when a man was riding hard, putting pressure on the cinches. Elwood imagined taking a spill at top speed. There would be a good chance of getting hurt.

He stood up, pulling the saddle blanket loose and stepping back. He shook out the blanket, doubled it even, and draped it onto the horse's back. Still with his free hand he unwrapped the latigo to free the front cinch and set it aside. With that done, he grabbed the saddle by the horn and swung the outfit so that the stirrups, latigo, and rear cinch sailed clear as he settled the seat into place. Then he picked up the front cinch and went to the off side to fix things. Using one half of the broken strap, he bored a new hole with his pocketknife and folded the piece into a much shorter billet than before. With that he had to tie the belly cinch high on the off side, and with the cinch now off-center, he was able to run the latigo around only once before he snugged it and held it in place with the spike of the cinch ring.

After buckling the rear cinch, he checked the front cinch for tightness by poking two fingers between the webbing and the horse's ribs. He led the animal out on a small circle, checked the cinch again, and mounted. He stood in the stirrups, shifted his weight to either side, and stood up straight. Nothing gave. He didn't like the idea of having the cinch off-center and the latigo that long with only one wrap, but everything felt tight enough that he was confident he could get back to the ranch.

He reined the speckled horse around and gave him a nudge. The horse picked up a fast walk and headed for the home corral. Elwood patted the animal's neck. It was just as well that horses didn't think about things like this. Elwood, on the other hand, couldn't think of much else. He could picture someone's hand holding a small knife and cutting the leather. The person had made a careful cut—not so much that the strap would break right away, and not so little that the strap would last a while. Elwood shook his head. This wasn't just some jolly puncher's idea of a joke or a prank, though he could imagine someone laughing at the result.

Elwood took a hand in the bunkhouse poker game that evening. Crandall sat at his left, followed by Foster, Merriman, and then Beckwith around on his right.

Crandall dealt the first hand. As he picked up his five cards and spread them for a peek, he said, "Five-card draw?"

"That's what we agreed on," said Beckwith in his dry voice.

"Sure we don't want to play low-hand-wins?"

"Just deal 'em."

Crandall folded his cards together, laid them on the table in front of him, and set a red chip on top. "Cards?"

"What's your hurry?" Beckwith closed his cards and held them with both hands. "Let's have a round of betting."

"You must have a better hand than I do."

It was open or fold, so Foster bet a nickel. Merriman called. Beckwith called and raised a nickel.

Elwood opened his cards and read them again. A pair of sixes, a deuce, a jack, and a king. He rode along for two nickels.

Crandall folded his hand and picked up the deck. "Cards?"

Foster took three, Merriman took one, and Beckwith took two. Elwood thought about keeping the king for a kicker, but after a second of deciding, he discarded three and kept the pair of sixes. In return he got an eight, a nine, and a king. The king was the third card, so he wouldn't have paired up with either of the first two cards anyway.

Foster passed, and Merriman passed. Beckwith bet a dime, and Elwood folded. Foster called. Merriman folded.

Beckwith showed three queens, a four, and a seven. Foster didn't have to show his hand, but he flipped it over anyway to show two fives and two jacks.

Crandall said, "Feevers and hooks. You had it won goin' in."

Beckwith shrugged as he raked in the small pile of chips. "Gotta play 'em," he said.

The deal passed to Foster, and the game went on. The second hand didn't last long, either, but the next hand did. Elwood folded, but the other four men stayed in for two rounds of betting before the draw and another two rounds after.

Beckwith won again. As he dragged the chips, Crandall spoke up in his usual tone of the good-humor man.

"What have you got goin' for you tonight?"

Beckwith tipped his head to the side. "Just lucky, I guess."

"Did you sneak off to town and change your luck?"

"Have to go to Fetterman for that. Got women to do the trick for soldiers." Beckwith's face had the expression of suppressing a smile. He left the chips in a loose pile and leaned forward to gather the cards for his deal.

"Speakin' of luck," said Elwood. "I had a bit of bad luck today."

"What kind?" said Beckwith. His hands did not pause, and his eyes did not look up.

"Broke a cinch."

"Huh."

"Actually it was the strap on the other side, where it rides in the D-ring."

Beckwith gave him a glance and went back to settling the cards into a deck for shuffling. "Glad you got back all right."

"Oh, it wasn't that much trouble. Like I said, just a little bit. The good luck was that we weren't goin' very fast."

"We?" Beckwith cracked the cards on the tabletop to even the deck.

"Me and the horse."

Crandall's voice came up on Elwood's left. "Where did it happen?"

Elwood decided to make him work for it. "Goin' down a draw."

"No, I mean, where at?"

"Oh, about ten miles out."

Beckwith spoke across the table in the cross tone he always used with Crandall. "What's it matter? The good thing is, he wasn't hurt."

"Would have been a long walk back," said Crandall.

Beckwith's brows tightened as he gave Crandall a stern look.

"That's right," said Elwood. "So I guess I was lucky in two ways. One, I wasn't going very fast, and two, I didn't have to walk back."

Crandall showed his crusty yellow teeth as he opened his mouth in a smile. "Maybe you're the one that went to town to change his luck."

"Fetterman's too far," said Elwood.

Crandall leaned back and tipped his chair. "Yeah, and your cinch might have given out on the way."

Elwood caught a glance of Beckwith, whose close-set eyes were glaring at Crandall. Elwood felt as if he could read the man's mind: *Don't you ever know when to shut up?*

The sun was beginning to slip in the afternoon sky when Elwood tied the dark horse in front of the general store. His boot heels sounded as he walked across the board sidewalk and into the store. The bell on the door tinkled, and he heard movement in the back of the store. Recalling where he had found the leather laces and straps on an earlier occasion, he went to that aisle. As he turned the corner at his end, he saw Sylvie Lamarre enter the aisle from the other end.

They met in the middle, in front of the display where Armitage had crowded him that day.

"Well, hello," she said. "Can I help you find something today?"

"I need some leather strap," he said. "Something like this." His eyes moved. "No, here it is. Already folded and punched." He took the leather between his thumb and forefinger. "That's good and thick."

"For a saddle."

"That's right. I had one break. Pretty rare, but it happened." He met her eyes. "All this stuff is important in its own way, you know."

"Oh, yes."

He took the billet from its peg and bent the double thickness. "This is good. Hard and tough." The smell of oil and new leather hung in the air, and he rubbed his thumb against his fingertips where a bit of the oily texture had stayed.

"And something else?"

"Yes," he said. "A pair of leather laces."

She made a small frown as she looked at his boots.

"Just for general purposes," he said. "Mending leather, tying things. Never know when you need it." He moved a couple of steps to his left. "Like these."

"Are those a good length? We've got longer ones."

"They should be fine. You usually cut off about a foot or less to tie something in place. So the overall length doesn't matter."

"Very well." She took a half step back. "Anything else?"

"Not today, I don't think."

She took the billet and the laces, and he followed her to the counter. "Do you need these wrapped?" she asked as she turned to face him.

"I can take them as they are." He laid a five-dollar gold piece on the counter.

She rang the cash box and gave him four silver dollars in change. "Thank you, Mr. Elwood."

He picked up the billet and the laces, and as he did so, he glanced around. Not seeing the store owner, he said, "Or El."

"Oh, yes. That's right." She flashed a smile.

"Thank you, Sylvie." He tipped his hat and smiled. "Hope to see you again soon."

"The same to you, El."

As he walked out of the store, he was conscious of her moving around to busy herself. The bell sounded as he went out, and he paused on the sidewalk to look around.

Not many people were on the street. The shadows had lengthened, and a few horses were tied up outside the Northern Star Saloon. Elwood stepped down from the sidewalk, spoke to the dark horse, and put his leather goods in the saddlebag. Looking again in the direction of the Northern Star, he figured he had time for one or two.

A crowd had begun to gather in the saloon. Tobacco smoke hung in a haze in the lamplight, and men's voices carried on the air. Elwood ordered a mug of beer at the bar and waited for it.

At his left, a man who had been leaning an elbow on the bar top and holding a drink in his free hand stood up and turned to him. The man had a flat-crowned hat with a concho hatband, and he wore a duster that looked like yellowed linen. He had creases at his eyes, a sagging mouth, and a soft, round belly. "Stranger here?"

"Not really," said Elwood. "I work at the Crown Butte Ranch, and I make it into town once in a while." He laid a dollar on the bar and reached for his mug. After taking a sip he said, "Name's Elwood. They call me El."

"Elwood what?"

"It's my last name."

"No, I meant Ell would what? Ell would kiss the girls an' make 'em cry? Ha-ha-ha." The man's laugh sounded mechanical.

"I'd need to know more girls."

"So would we all." The man opened his mouth, showing his tongue where it lay against his lower teeth, and he gave a longer version of his artificial laugh. "Ha-ha-ha-ha, ha-ha-ha-ha-ha, ha-ha-ha." He shifted his glass of whiskey to his left hand and held out his right. "Name's Angell Gunn."

Elwood shook his hand and said, "Pleased to meet you."

The other man took a drink and gave a self-satisfied smile. "Angell was muh mother's last name. With two ells. And Gunn was muh father's. That's how I come to make a joke about the ell."

"I see."

"When the wimmen ask me, I tell 'em I might be more Gunn than Angell." He gave a provocative hip movement made worse by the motion of his round little belly. "What would I tell 'em if muh folks had named me Peter?" Then came the laugh, like a mechanical windup toy.

Elwood did not say anything. He took a drink of beer and thought about how good it tasted.

"So you're a ranch hand, uh?"

"That's right."

"Good as anything." Angell Gunn raised his glass to his lips, and his wrinkled neck moved as he downed a swallow of whiskey. He licked his lips and said, "Me, I'm in business for myself."

Elwood nodded.

"When I make a deal, I make a deal. I've bought and sold everything from parrots and pianos to houses and hotels to skyscrapers in the canyons of Chicago."

"That's quite a bit." Elwood tipped up his mug.

"I don't ask another man his business, and I don't tell him mine. But if I make a deal, it sticks. I don't cross no one, and no one crosses me." He doubled his fist and gave a short, tight jab in the air in front of his soft belly. With a hard stare he added, "Men are better off not havin' to learn it, but I'm a tough son of a bitch."

Elwood set his mug on the bar. "Does it go that far when someone's sellin' parrots and pianos?"

Angell Gunn's mouth lifted in what passed for a wry smile. "That's city stuff. I said I sold it." His mouth lifted again. "Not all business is sales."

"Oh, no doubt." Elwood reached for his beer and saw that the mug was half-full. He had to decide between enjoying his drink at leisure or getting away from his new acquaintance. He drank about half of what was left.

Angell Gunn cleared his throat and made a "heh-heh" sound. Then he said, "Not everyone's cut out for business."

Elwood pushed out his lower lip and shook his head.

"Someone like yourself, for instance. There's a need for men to work for wages." He raised his head and glanced down, as if he was looking through half-lens glasses. "Buy you a drink?"

"No, thanks. I've got to be going." Elwood drank the rest of his beer.

"Next time." The man held out his hand. "Angell Gunn."

"Elwood."

"I'll remember it. You work for the Copper Butte Ranch."

"Crown Butte."

"That's right." The man gave his self-satisfied smile and patted Elwood on the shoulder. "Keep up the good work, partner."

Elwood wondered where the man would have gotten any idea of what quality of work Elwood did. "Thanks," he said, "and good luck to you."

"Good luck's half the game." Angell Gunn gave the motion of doubling his fist and stopping it in a quick jerk. "The other half's knowin' what to do and when to do it." He opened his mouth, and his tongue lay flat in the bottom. "Except with the women. Then it's all luck. Ha-ha-ha-ha, ha-ha-ha-ha, ha-ha-ha, ha-ha."

Elwood set his empty mug on the bar, and for the first time in a few minutes he glanced around the saloon. Josh Armitage, shining in his black vest and knee-high boots, stood near the front door. His eyes moved away from Elwood, and he wandered toward a poker table. Elwood headed for the door and walked out into the evening air. There had been a moment when he thought about asking Ned the bartender if had heard anything new about D. W. Stanley, but with the appearance of Angell Gunn and then Josh Armitage, that moment was long gone.

Rand Sullivan hung his hat on a peg and sat down at the table. The bunkhouse men had just finished breakfast and were drinking coffee. Otis passed an empty cup down the table, and Elwood handed the coffeepot across. Beckwith pushed back his chair, hiked up a leg, and began to roll a cigarette.

As the boss poured himself a cup he said, "What's new this morning?"

Al Foster, said, "George was just showing us a tooth he lost."

Sullivan arched his eyebrows. "Is that right, George? You must not have lost it for long if you still have it."

Crandall had taken out his tobacco pouch and was opening it. He put on a slow grin and said, "I had it pulled a couple of years ago. It was mine, so I kept it."

"Men do that." Sullivan drank from his coffee. "I knew a man had a finger cut off, and he carried it around, all shriveled up and in a Bull Durham sack."

Crandall wagged his head to each side. "They carry around all kinds of stuff. Got their souvenirs and good-luck charms. Me, I think I'd just as soon have a rabbit's foot as a shriveled old finger." His mouth opened in a grin again. "Of course, if it was my finger, I might not want to part with it."

"You'd have it right in there with your tooth," said Beckwith. "Have a collection to build on."

No one spoke for a few seconds. Sullivan cleared his throat and said, "Well, it's all a cheery subject. To move on to another, El, I haven't heard anything of Norville since we got done with roundup. I don't know if he's still there. I thought I might have you take a ride over and see."

"Shall I take along some grub? I should have brought him some coffee last time as well."

"It wouldn't hurt." The boss nodded toward the cook. "Otis can give you something."

Otis looked up and around. "There went the apple pie I was savin'."

"What?" said Crandall. He was lifting tobacco from his pouch, and he paused with his mouth open.

"Just kidding. I don't have any pie. But I can send some biscuits, and maybe some raisins like before."

Norville's place lay south and west, so Elwood had the sun at his back as he topped the last rise and gave the speckled horse a rest. He reached forward to separate a tangle in the gray mane. The horse shifted on its feet, and a minute later it gave a long snuffle. Elwood gave it rein and headed down the slope.

Nothing had changed in the layout of the ranch yard, but the bay horse was not in the corral, and two horses stood in front of the house. A man stood with them.

Elwood took it slow, trying to make out the man and the horses, but he didn't recognize anything at a distance. The man stood and gazed at him for a moment, then turned his back and paid no attention. A dark space showed where the door of the white ranch house was open.

The sun was warming the day, and no breeze stirred. Elwood rode within a hundred yards, then fifty, and the man stayed between the two horses, patting their necks and lifting their front feet.

Elwood brought his horse to a stop and called out, "Anyone home?"

The man emerged from between the two horses and turned to face Elwood. All the details filled in at once—a short, husky man with reddish-brown hair, a muddy complexion, and a pink nose.

Driggs brushed his hand across the handle of his six-gun and tipped his hat against the sun. His gravelly voice came out of the shadow of the brim. "You get around."

"I could say the same for you."

"What do you need?"

"I came to see Norville."

"He ain't here."

Elwood swung down and held onto his reins. He imagined Driggs had recognized the pale, speckled horse with the gray mane and tail. He also imagined that Driggs's partner, Haden, was prowling in the house, and he didn't like the idea. "How do you come to be here?" he asked.

"Got more business than you do."

Elwood felt his blood rising, and he made himself stay calm. A memory of Angell Gunn flickered in his mind, and he said, "There's lots of different kinds of business."

"And some of it's none of yours."

Elwood had an urge to land a fist on the man's pink nose, but he didn't see much purpose to it, and he didn't like the odds of one man against two with no one else around. "My boss sent me here," he said.

"So did mine."

"I didn't know you had a job."

Driggs took a step forward. "Huh. You'd like to try to get me fired again."

"Oh, go on. I just wonder why you'd be out here nosin' around if you've got a job to do."

A voice came from the doorway. "What's goin' on?"

Elwood didn't recognize the voice right away, nor did he recognize the man who stood in the shadow. Then the details materialized, and they were not of the man Elwood expected to see with Driggs. The figure in the shaded doorway was dark because the man wore a black hat, a black vest, a charcoal gray shirt, and dark pants tucked into knee-high black boots.

Driggs turned to Armitage and said, "Got a visitor."

Armitage moved out onto the doorstep, and the ivory handle of his six-gun caught the sunlight. "Oh, it's you," he said. "What do you want?"

"Sullivan sent me to check on Norville. We hadn't heard from him in a while."

"He's not here anymore. He sold the place."

Elwood thought for a moment as he phrased his question. "Do you know where he is?"

"He's not dead yet, if that's what you mean. Or at least he wasn't last week. They've got him in a place in North Platte. One of those where they give you plenty of morphine."

Elwood took a quick glance at the house and corrals, things that a man had worked for and had to give up. "So Jennings bought it?"

"That's right."

"Where's he?"

Armitage took out a pocketknife and began to clean his fingernails. "For as much as it's any of your business, he's back in Pennsylvania."

"I thought my boss might like to know."

"Everyone likes to know something. What else would you like to ask?"

"That's probably enough for today."

Armitage clicked the knife shut and put it away. "Just fine. Give my regards to your boss."

"Thanks. And the same to yours." Elwood turned to Driggs. "And yours." Elwood turned the pale horse and walked it out a few steps, checked to see that his cinch was tight, then flipped his reins into place and mounted up. Armitage and Driggs stood watching as he rode away.

Rand Sullivan rapped his pipe upside down on the corral post when Elwood finished with his report. "I guess that's the way it goes," the boss said. "Nothing is forever. I feel sorry for Norville, but at least he's not dead yet, and he got more of a chance than some men do." Sullivan brushed the cinders off the top of the post. "I can't say I'm delighted that Jennings bought the place."

"Or that he's got that fellow Driggs workin' for him."

"We don't get to choose those things. Just keep our eyes open more than ever, and maybe we'll be able to catch someone at something." Sullivan gazed at the buttes in the distance, where the sun was about to touch. "Oh, by the way," he said. "This came for you." He reached inside his vest and drew out an envelope. "It was in a letter addressed to my wife. She asked that I pass it on."

Elwood's pulse quickened when he saw the handwriting on the envelope. Only two words appeared—"Mr. Elwood"—but he knew who had written them.

The boss smiled, gave a firm nod, and walked away. Elwood broke the wax seal and took out the letter. As he unfolded it, more of her handwriting came into view.

Dear El:

This is just a short note for the moment, to let you know that I have overcome the difficulties that presented themselves a while back. I remain determined to put distance between myself and those things that impede me. To that end, I am planning another visit to my dear friend Ellen and the environs of the Crown Butte Ranch. I hope you are not too mortified by this news, but even if you are, I hope we can at least be on friendly terms in passing. Thus I remain

In friendship,
Josie

Elwood read the letter a second and a third time, noting the reserved tone and taking care not to find more intention than was expressed. He could have wished for a little more of a personal touch or even a little more humor, but the word "mortified" did well enough. Was he mortified? He hoped not.

Chapter Eight

Elwood lay on his stomach, looking through the binoculars at the clear images of grass, sagebrush, and rocks. A small commotion made him turn around. The sorrel with the light-colored mane and tail had kicked at a horsefly and was now whipping its tail. The big insect rose, went out on a circle, and came back to land on the horse's neck. The sorrel rippled its muscles, and the fly lifted, only to land again a few inches away. Elwood got up with the neck rope in his hand, took careful steps toward the horse, and slapped the fly. The bug fell in the dirt, squirming, a gray-and-black pest as big as the last joint of a man's finger. It turned as if it was ready to rise again, so Elwood stepped on it and rotated his foot to grind it into the dirt.

A dry breeze came up from the shallow basin in front of him, rippling across the grass that had begun to dry in midsummer. Elwood wondered how many calves or even older stock had been spirited off in that direction, following one trail or another through the land formations to the west. Rand Sullivan had a lot of patience, but as he himself had said, letting a couple of men go would only leave them free to do more of the same. If he kept them on, sooner or later he might find the connection and catch someone else as well. Even at that, Elwood wondered how much longer Beckwith and Crandall would last at the Crown Butte Ranch.

Elwood coiled the neck rope and tied it to his saddle. The sorrel's honey-colored mane lifted in the breeze, and the horse turned its head. Elwood patted the velvety nose. Some horses, like some dogs, seemed to be pure of heart, with not a bit of guile in them. He had heard the theory that all babies were born that way, but he had seen some pretty small kids who already had the tinctures of malice and envy and deceit running through them. When they were old enough to make it on their own, they were a long ways away from having a pure heart, if they ever did.

The combination of Driggs and Armitage came back to him. Jennings had his place farther west, and that was the general direction where Elwood had imagined Driggs was hanging out when Beckwith and Crandall were staying at the line shack. As he reviewed things now, Elwood recalled Crandall telling Armitage about Driggs and Haden, and then Armitage saying he would be on the lookout for them. Something like that. And then he went and hired Driggs, from the looks of it, and probably Haden. Well, that was Armitage. He had a high opinion of himself, and he would assume that no common hand like Driggs was going to put something over on him.

Elwood took a last lingering gaze at the land to the west, then led out the sorrel with the light mane and tail shining in the sun. He checked the cinch for tightness, mounted up, and rode away.

Shadows were stretching across the ranch yard as Elwood came in from his day's ride. He dismounted in front of the barn and led the sorrel inside. There he took off the saddle and blanket, slipped off the bridle, and brushed the horse. As he turned the sorrel into the pen, he saw that the trough had water and the other horses were eating hay, so the chores were done.

He paused on his way out the barn door. The buckboard was not in the same place as it had been in the morning, and he had just seen the wagon horses eating with the other horses that had done a day's work. Someone might have gone to town.

Inside the bunkhouse, supper had not yet hit the table. Otis was busy at the stove, and Beckwith was reading an almanac. Elwood fancied that the close-set eyes were searching for the next rustler's moon.

Crandall had Foster and Merriman as an audience at the table. "Cut the deck, look at the card, and don't show it to me. Good. Now put it back." Crandall took the cards. "Now we've got it buried in the middle of the deck. I cut the deck one, two, three times. Shuffle. Now I tap the deck." Crandall snapped the top card and held it up. "Is this your card?"

Elwood washed up and pulled a chair out from the table. He felt a great temptation to ask Otis if someone had gone to town, but he kept the question to himself and sat down.

"See anything today?" asked Crandall.

Beckwith looked up without raising his head.

"Nothing out of the ordinary," Elwood answered. "How about yourself?"

"Nothin' new."

Beckwith's eyes went back to his almanac.

Crandall affected an air of nonchalance as he cracked the deck, split it with a snap and a flutter, and shuffled the two halves together. "I guess I did see one thing."

Beckwith looked up. Foster and Merriman waited. Otis banged a metal spoon on the lid of a pot.

Crandall looked around. "Oh, it was nothin' that important. Just a big ol' ratt-ler, thick as my wrist, halfway down a prairie-dog hole." He shrugged. "I guess everything's got to make a livin'. Everything's that's got a gullet has got to put somethin' down it."

"Dangerous stuff," said Otis as he set a pot on the table. "That's how men choke."

Crandall laughed. "Sure. I heard of a fella in the penitentiary.

He choked on a towel. They said he did it to himself. Can you believe it? I couldn't. I think they just wanted to close the book on him. But you're right, Otis. Men can choke on a piece of steak, or a chicken bone."

"People choke on their own words," said Beckwith. He closed the almanac and set it to one side on the table.

"That just goes to show, there's more than one way to do things." Crandall set the deck aside. "That was about as big a ratt-ler as I've seen in this country. Like they say, the big fish eats the little fish. If I didn't know better, it looked like the hole in the ground was swallowin' the snake."

Beckwith spoke again. "That's another line of work you could go into."

"What's that? A scientist?"

"No. A snake swallower. But just be careful you don't end up like your friend with the towel."

"He was no friend of mine." Then, as if he wished for once that he had said less than he did, Crandall added, "It was just a story I heard."

Beckwith was a picture of self-restraint as he took in a long breath through his nose. Elwood was sure the man had something more to say, but he granted Beckwith the good judgment of not giving Crandall the chance of saying even more.

Dusk was settling as Elwood stepped out of the bunkhouse and closed the door behind him. If she was here, as he had the feeling that she was, and if she wanted to see him, she would be on the lookout.

He set off at a slow pace, readjusting his hat and brushing his sleeves. He sauntered toward the barn but kept the ranch house at the corner of his vision. Nothing stirred. He wandered past the barn, came back, turned again, and stopped to lean with his forearms on the edge of the wagon box. Maybe she had ridden in this wagon today, but maybe it had held nothing more alive than sacks of beans and flour.

His thoughts drifted to Crandall's story about the snake to his own speculation about Armitage and Driggs to the odd meeting with Angell Gunn. Now there was someone with a digestive tract. Of course, everyone had one, but it seemed more prominent in some people. Range riders didn't get a soft belly like that, not until they hung up their spurs and took to indoor work or no work at all.

A voice floated on the air and made his pulse jump. "Hello, stranger."

He turned and saw her walking toward him, a light figure in the dusk. "Hello," he said. As she came closer, he saw that she was wearing a tan dress with her hair loose and touching the collar. Her complexion was light as always, and her hair had a lighter tone than he remembered. She held her hands out and he took them, but he did not draw her to him, and she did not move forward on her own.

"I wasn't sure if you would want to see me," she said.

"Of course I did." As he said it, he wondered if he let himself sound too eager.

"I'm sorry I left the way I did."

"It's all right," he said. "I got through it."

"There was no good way to do it."

"Sometimes there's not a good way, I suppose." He found her eyes. "It's hard to believe you're back."

She tightened her hands in his. "Well, I am. See? That's proof."

"Yes, it is." He relaxed his hands.

"Did you want to say something?"

"I don't know," he said.

"Go ahead. No one's in a hurry, I hope. I'm not."

He took in a full breath and relaxed. His heartbeat had settled down. "Well, I don't know where to start. As far as that goes, I'm not sure where we are. But I don't take anything for granted."

"Neither do I. No assumptions." Her eyes held steady. "I'm sorry if I hurt you, and I wouldn't blame you if—"

"I don't hurt that easy. It's in the past. We're in the present." He let her hands go.

"That's right," she said. "Here and now. Shall we walk?"

"Why not?"

She turned, and he fell in beside her. They walked past the ranch house toward the open country where they had walked on another night earlier in the year. A faint breeze carried the scent of her perfume, reminiscent of lilac blossoms. For a moment he had the illusion that lilacs were still in bloom and time had not passed.

When they were a good hundred yards out, he spoke. "I was glad to get your letter. Not only to know you were coming out again, but to know you were going to be able to live on your own terms the way you want to."

"It's been a struggle," she said. "If I hadn't gone when I did, he might have made charges of abandonment, which wouldn't have helped my case at all. As it turned out, my going back gave me the opportunity to document some things myself."

"Things about him."

"Yes. About him. It took some doing. I had to get up some resolve. And it took resources." She paused.

"You mean money."

"Yes. I had to come up with some money, which I was able to do, and I had to have some dealings, though indirectly, with investigators who could collect the proof." She paused again for a few seconds, and her voice picked up as she said, "But I got it. The infidelities, the physical treatment of me—he's quite finished, and he knows it."

"That's a big step, if you can hang onto it."

"Oh, I know. I've heard plenty of stories. They repent, they let things blow over, they use every leverage they can. But not this one. Not anymore."

Elwood took a few seconds to build himself up for the next question. "So you didn't come out here to get away from him again?"

"No," she said, in a methodical tone. "I've already done that. Now I've come out here to think things through in these great wide open spaces." She looked up. "I thought I remembered how wonderful this sky was, but one's memory can't come close to the real thing."

He felt left out, but he reminded himself he was making no assumptions. "I suppose we get used to it," he said, "but I'm sure I'd miss it if I had to go somewhere else."

"Why would you have to? You don't have anything to run from, do you?"

"Oh, no. But bein' a hired man on horseback isn't a good prospect forever. At some point, a man might look for other opportunities, and he doesn't know where they might take him. Not that I see myself raisin' hogs in Missouri or runnin' a millinery shop in Ohio."

She laughed. "I don't quite see you doing those things, either."

"For the time being, I don't have plans to do anything different from what I'm doing now. Do my work as well as I can, and put a little money by so if a change does come up, I won't be too broke to manage it."

"Well, I was glad to find you here when I got back. Not that I expected you to be gone, but it was reassuring all the same."

"Thanks. By the way, I was amused by what you called me. You said, 'Hello, stranger.' "

"Oh, that's just an expression. You've heard it before, haven't you?"

"Plenty of times. Just that hearing it from you was, I don't know, cheerful. Made me feel that things hadn't changed all that much."

"Not in terms of confidence, if that's what you mean. Of course, other things have changed."

"Of course. But that's what I meant. I was afraid you might be distant."

"Did my letter give you that idea?"

"No," he said, "but it didn't keep me from wondering if things were going to be . . . strained."

"Oh, I'm sorry. I suppose I was trying not to be too forward."

"It's all right. No harm done." He paused. "There was another thing I wanted to say." He paused again, and when she didn't speak, he went on. "While you were gone, I heard a song that really struck me. I was in an establishment one night, and there was a man and a woman singing a song. It was about a fella who meets a girl, and she lives on the other side of the mountain. She tells him, 'Don't be a stranger. Come and see me when you can.' "

"That sounds like a charming song."

"It was. The woman had a beautiful voice. Full of feeling. Sad, but in a way that makes you like it."

"Sentimental."

"I suppose so. Anyway, when the boy gets some time off, he rides over the mountain to see her, and he finds out she's married someone else. So he rides back home, singing her words to console himself."

"Well, that does sound sentimental. Like all those sad ballads." She paused and said, "Is that how you thought of me?"

"I must say I felt some similarities."

"That's what some of those sad songs are for."

"And I must admit, I sang those words to myself a few times, and they did seem to work like a kind of medicine."

"Oh, so you remembered the song well enough to sing it?"

"Just the chorus. The part the woman sang. It was shorter, but it had a lot to it."

"Could you sing it now? I'd love to hear it."

"Oh, no. I don't sing worth a—not well at all."

She laid her hand on his forearm. "Oh, please sing it. There's no one around."

"I don't know. I—"

She applied light pressure to his arm. "Don't be self-conscious. It's just a few lines from a song."

"Oh, all right." He took a breath to calm himself, and in the solitude of nighttime on the rangeland, he went out of himself and into the song he had sung so many times when he was alone.

Darlin', don't be a stranger
When time is on your hands.
You're just one range over
In a large and lonesome land.

It takes a bit of courage
If you're a worthy man,
So don't be a stranger,
Come and see me when you can.

"That was wonderful," she said.

"The woman sang it much better, I'll say that. She put a lot of feeling into it, and like I said, I carried it around with me and used it like medicine when I got to feeling down."

She pressed his arm again. "Of course you were sad. What else could I expect? It's a wonder you wanted to see me again."

"I couldn't have wanted otherwise."

She laughed. "So you could tell me about the song."

"Well, I did have it in mind that if I ever saw you again, I'd tell you about it. But I hoped there would be more to our conversation than that." His eyes met hers in the moonlight. "And you? Did you have anything specific in mind if we ever saw each other again?"

"Do you really want to know?"

"Of course I do."

Her eyes held steady as she said, "I told myself I was going to make it up to you."

With those words he was lost in a swirl, taking her in his arms as his eyes closed and their lips met. From the way she held him in return, he knew he was no stranger in her arms.

Elwood tied up the pale horse outside the barn and brushed it. As always, the gray speckles seemed to have soaked into the off-white coat, and they stayed put as he brushed out the dust and loose hair. Changing the brush for the steel comb, he pulled the tangles out of the gray mane and tail.

Movement caught his eye as the door of the ranch house opened and Josephine came out wearing a light-blue dress and carrying a parasol. Elwood took up the brush again and gave the horse a few more swipes as he gave her time to approach.

"Good afternoon," she said. "Do you always change horses at midday?"

"When we come back. Sometimes we stay out."

"Of course."

"And how are you today?"

"Just fine," she said. "And you?"

"Doin' well." He picked up the near hoof and looked at the underside. "By the way," he said, "there's something I've been wondering for a while."

"And what's that?"

"Have you ever known, or heard of, a man named D. W. Stanley?"

Her face held a thoughtful expression for a moment. She shook her head and said, "No. Is there some reason I might?"

"Not really. It was just a guess on my part, and probably not a good one. Poor fellow was traveling through here, and he died in town. We knew him because he spent a night here at the ranch."

"Poor man. It's too bad." Her face clouded. "Was that all there was to it?"

"Oh, I left out the reason I asked. When he died, they found a train ticket from Cheyenne to Omaha in his effects."

She tipped her head side-to-side beneath the parasol. "Well, a good many people travel to there, and it's a big city. It's not Chicago, of course, but it's big enough that one knows very few people in comparison with the multitudes that one doesn't know."

"How about a man called Jim Farley?"

"That's a common enough name, but it doesn't call to mind anyone in particular."

"Or Jude Ostrander?"

"No, that one's singular enough that I would remember it. Who are these two?"

"Reportedly the same person, and according to the late Mr. Stanley, something of a crook."

Josephine laughed. "And you think I would have heard of him through my husband?"

"Well, it was worth a try."

"What sort of commerce does he work in?"

"Strictly what I heard, and not anything I would claim to know myself, but robbing banks."

She laughed again. "That's a bit strong for Alex. I'm quite sure he's had some shady deals, but they've all been related to grain brokering. Not that it couldn't run to large sums, but it's not on the same level as robbing banks." She took on a more serious tone. "Am I to understand that there was some connection between the reputed bank robber and the man who died?"

"I don't know. This man who called himself Jim Farley disappeared, and a couple of days later, Mr. Stanley was found dead. This all happened when you were here before, at about the time you were having correspondence and telegrams with Mr. Newton, and not long before he came out here himself. At least as I understand it, he did."

"Yes, he did. But I don't think there's anything more than a coincidence. Things happen close together in time."

"That, and the train ticket. Just enough to make me wonder. And ask."

"No harm in that," she said. Then, with a change in tone that went along with a change in subject, she said, "I've had that song going through my head. The one you sang."

"I'm afraid I don't sing very well."

"You did fine."

"At least it was only two verses."

Josephine held onto her parasol as she turned toward the buttes. "So she was one range over. Would it be out that way?"

"In the song, yes. In reality, there's just other ranches out there." He was on the verge of saying, "And rustlers, too," but he checked himself.

"Is that where you ride?"

"I go out to the west as much as anywhere else, and lately I've gone there more. Keep an eye on things, see if any cows or calves need lookin' after."

"And when do you go out on roundup again? Rand says it's in the fall."

"In about six weeks. Late September, early October."

"You get into cold weather by then, don't you?"

"Sometimes. But the flies aren't so bad. We get our first frost about then, and the weather varies after that."

"I noticed on the way from town that the grass is turning dry. It was so green when I left. Yet it seems as if I was gone but a day or two."

"Yes, it does." He wanted to ask her if she planned to stay through the fall, but he had conditioned himself not to ask any questions that touched upon intentions in that way. She had said she had come to think things through, and he did not want to crowd her.

"Time flies by," she said. "One has the fear of waking up someday in old age and wondering where the time all went."

"I've heard of that. Excuse me. I need to get my saddle."

When he came back, she watched as he laid the blanket and the saddle on the horse's back. She seemed to be waiting to speak again, and after a minute she said, "This is no time to be thinking of old age, is it? Getting there should be good enough. Gather the rosebuds in the meanwhile. I suppose you've heard that expression, too."

"Something like it." He ran the latigo through the cinch ring and pulled the slack.

"I've often thought of the wild roses you picked for me that day."

"I've remembered them, too." He pulled the latigo through again. "There's not much in bloom at this point in the summer."

"Oh, every season has its beauty."

He turned and gazed at her, a fair flower beneath the shade of the parasol. She stood but an arm's length away, and he could feel a current flowing between them. In a low voice he said, "I could kiss you right now, but I know I had better not."

She smiled as she tipped her head a few degrees. "I'll wait till you get back."

★ ★ ★ ★ ★

The dry wind from the west carried the smell of sagebrush as Elwood rode to the top of a hill between two clay bluffs. The horse's gray mane lifted in the breeze, and the horse snuffled.

"Easy, boy." Elwood held the saddle horn and slid down light and soft. He patted the horse's cheek and rubbed his hand over the velvety nose. Pulling down on the reins, he made the horse move back so he could step in front. He walked forward a few yards, picking his way through the rocks and letting the horse do the same.

The rangeland ahead came into view. A valley of sagebrush, cactus, and grass, rougher grazing than the grassland closer to the ranch, ran north and south with dull-colored buttes on either side. Elwood had heard that if a man knew the way, as some horse thieves did, he could ride fifty miles from north to south through this maze of buttes. He also knew there were trails through to the west, passages less well known than the two main roads that ran ten miles north of here and twenty miles south. But he was yet to find one that showed the kind of wear he was looking for.

He had also heard of outlaw hideouts, with sentinels and secret entryways, but he had never seen any evidence. Although he had been through this maze several times, he knew, as with the rest of the butte country, there were canyons and pockets and valleys he had not seen, as well as others he was seeing again as if for the first time.

He led the horse the rest of the way through the rocks and mounted up. After another sweeping glance of the little valley, he rode down the slope and into the open. With the breeze in his face he crossed the valley at a lope. He rode into shade when he reached the bluffs on the other side, and he turned to follow the trail along the base until he came to an opening between two formations. He rode in, and on a hunch he dismounted to take a look at his back trail. Keeping the pale horse out of sight, he sidestepped until he came to the edge of the opening.

The valley came into view, and he found the gap he had ridden through on the other side. The afternoon sun brightened the grass and dull-colored bluffs, and he blinked to let his eyes adjust. Then his eyes strained as he thought he saw motion. He blinked and peered again. This time he saw nothing, but he was sure he had seen the head and chest of a brownish horse.

He sagged back, waited a minute, and took another look. Again he saw nothing but the landscape. He tipped his head back and saw where the sun was. He had time to wait. If someone was following him, he would come this same way before long. Elwood glanced at his horse and again at the sun. He could wait, but he was going to have to stay out of sight and not let himself take a single peek. Just once could ruin it. He was going to have to sit here and make himself be patient. Maybe no one would come. But if someone did, Elwood might learn something.

His first guess was Driggs. Dogging him was the type of thing Driggs would do, with or without his boss's knowledge. Or it could be Haden. Elwood had lost track of him, though he imagined the man could still be working with his partner. Then there was Armitage himself, and Elwood couldn't discount either Beckwith or Crandall, although they were supposed to be working way over to the south.

He was just going to have to wait. Not five minutes had gone by, and he was already starting to sweat. He saw that he was in a pretty small area, with no air movement, and the sun beat down on him. If he moved to another spot at this point, someone might see him.

The pale horse shifted on its feet and let out a sigh. Elwood wiped his brow. Of all the places to hole up, he could have found one with some shade. He sat on a rock where he would be able to see a horse and rider as soon as they came through the gap. He took a long, deep breath and relaxed his eyes. He stretched. He yawned. He opened his eyes and let them close halfway again.

He imagined a horse and rider sauntering across the open area. With equal ease he imagined the valley and the bluffs on the other side with no one at all, just the grass and the sage and a few scattered rocks in the afternoon sun, and him sitting here sweating, waiting for nothing.

His head dipped, and he opened his eyes. He had dozed off. He shook his head, blinked, rubbed his nose. Sometimes, later in the summer, the buds on the sagebrush made him sneeze. He hoped it didn't happen today.

Time dragged on, and the sun did not seem to move. Elwood could not tell whether ten minutes had passed or half an hour. Closer to fifteen, he guessed. He had to wait at least that much longer. After half an hour, he could give it up.

The horse raised its head and turned it. Elwood listened. He thought he heard a sound coming through the earth, but it was very faint. There it was again. A few seconds later, he thought he heard the click of a piece of rock moving.

He held the reins short and put his hand over the horse's nose. Footfalls came one after another, and a man rode into view on a square-headed, muddy-colored horse.

Elwood did not recognize the rider at first. The man was taller than Driggs would be, and he wore a duster that didn't show much of a shape. He was holding onto his hat, which had a low brim and a flat crown. When the rider lowered his hand, Elwood saw the concho hatband as well as the sagging face of Angell Gunn.

Elwood's horse jerked its head up and whinnied. Angell Gunn's horse let out a grunt and a wheeze as the rider spurred it. A cloud of dust rose stirrup-high as the horse whirled and came to a stop. Angell Gunn slid off the other side and came up with a pistol barrel aimed across the saddle.

"What the hell you doin', boy?"

"Waitin'."

"Good way to get yourself shot. Waitin' for what? Christmas?"

"Waitin' to see who was followin' me."

The man's brown eyes bore down on Elwood from twenty feet away. "Be careful what you say and how you say it."

The dust was drifting away, but Elwood could smell it along with the odor of the horse. He said, "I thought I saw someone following me, so I waited to see who it was."

"Well, looka here. If you're out in front of someone, that's your business. And if there's someone out in front of you, that doesn't mean you're tailin' him."

Elwood didn't answer as the sun bore down.

Angell Gunn squinted and gave a condescending smile. "I mind my business, and I let others mind theirs. But by God, if someone's layin' in wait for me, I could put a hole in 'em and not think twice about it." The man tipped his head back as if he was giving an appraisal. He brought down the pistol and came out from behind the horse, putting the gun in his holster. He walked stiff-legged, and his soft belly was prominent. "I think I know you," he said. "Didn't I meet you a while back?"

"That's right. We met in the Northern Star. My name's Elwood."

"Oh, yeah. I remember. What would Elwood do? Ha-ha-ha-ha-ha. I didn't expect to see you out here, actin' like you were about to waylay me."

Elwood noticed a rifle stock and a leather scabbard snugged up to the saddle. "I didn't expect to see you, as far as that goes."

"Who did you expect to see? Lily of the West? Ha-ha-ha-ha-ha."

Elwood smiled. "I don't know her."

"Neither do I. Just heard about her in a song. But you're as likely to meet her out here as you are to have me followin' you."

"That's good to know." Elwood looked up at the sun. "Well, the day's gettin' on, and I don't like to crowd anyone. I'll let you go on your way here, tend to your business, and it's about time for me to head back to the ranch anyway."

A smile lifted on the man's face. "You wouldn't think about followin' old Angell Gunn, would you?"

Elwood smiled in return. "Not at all. You've got a better chance of seeing Lily of the West."

"Ha-ha-ha-ha-ha. If she shows up, I've got somethin' for her."

"Well, so long, then." Elwood tugged on the reins and led the pale horse toward the trail both men had ridden in on.

"You bet," said Angell Gunn. "We'll see you again."

Elwood did not look back as he took the horse through the gap and swung aboard. He rode out of the shadows and felt the sun on his back and the breeze on the side of his face. He had half a mind to wait and see how long it took Angell Gunn to turn around and head for town, but he had said he was going back to the ranch, and it didn't seem like a bad idea.

Chapter Nine

Elwood and Josephine walked along the top of the bluff where he had taken her, Mrs. Sullivan, and the children to look for tepee rings and arrowheads back in the springtime. The day being Sunday and work not pressing, they enjoyed the time off with a midday walk. The weather was sunny and cloudless with a dry breeze lifting from the east. Grasshoppers skittered ahead of them in the drying grass. Out of habit, Elwood kept an eye out for snakes.

"It's hard to believe I've been here two weeks already," she said. "This landscape seems so constant, so timeless. And yet times goes on."

"It does. And the sunny season doesn't last all that long. You might find the cold weather a good subject for your philosophical turn of mind."

"Oh, I've seen winter and bitter cold, believe me. Omaha is not the southern coast."

"I don't know if you get the wind where you come from. We do here. Wind in all seasons, it seems, but especially bad in November. It blows for days, dreary enough to take the cheer right out of you."

"I've seen wind, of course, but I can't say I've seen what you describe." She smiled. "Perhaps I'll be able to tell you later."

They walked along for a moment without speaking. Elwood imagined she might be thinking along the same lines he was, but as she kept to herself, he decided to go ahead. "Not wishin' to be too forward, and not assumin' that we have to be that definite at this point, I can't help wonderin' if you have an idea of how long you might stay this time."

"Of course you have every right to wonder, and I wish I had a more definite course of action to declare." She gave a light laugh. "I'd like to say I'm going through a period of indecision, but really, I've been doing that for a long time and don't see an immediate end to it."

"I take it you mean indecision about what you're going to do, not what you have done. What I mean is, you aren't still indecisive about your, um, Mr. Newton, are you?"

"Oh, no. That's done. I'm quite sure I can say that much with certainty. We've dug the grave there. Found a fitting place." After a pause she said, "You don't happen to know that poem, do you?"

"I'm afraid I don't. I read some of the poets at one time, but I don't recall those words."

"You wouldn't have read him in school. His name is George Meredith. He's British, and he wrote a series of poems called 'Modern Love.' And they are quite modern. In this one he writes, 'Here is a fitting place to dig Love's grave.' Very resolved, not sentimental at all. He goes on, 'I see no sin. The wrong is mixed.' You see what I mean by modern? He's not looking to find blame. Instead, he writes, 'We are betrayed by what is false within.' " She held her hand at chest level in an open gesture. "Now I find that very realistic, very accepting of what the situation is. Spells it out quite clearly that what's done is done. Once one knows and accepts that truth, there's no going back."

"He must have known what he was talking about."

"I should say. He was friends with a painter, and he posed as the model for a very successful painting. Then his wife ran off with the painter. Had quite an effect on him."

"I can imagine it would."

"But he got over it. I'm sure that writing the poems helped him. Then the poems in turn might help someone else. Rather like that song you told me about. I think you said it was like medicine. That's the way these poems work, though not really like medicine because they don't cure anything. But they help a person see. And ponder it. 'We are betrayed by what is false within.' It gives one a great deal to think about."

Elwood didn't know if she was expressing a kind of intellectual superiority or if she was making a defense. So he said, "Not very forward-looking in itself, but I suppose it helps."

"Oh, yes. If you can get a grasp on things, have an idea of where you are and why the things happened that got you there, then you can move ahead."

"And that's more or less where you are?"

She laughed, again in a light, airy way. "I would be contradicting myself if I said no. So, yes, I imagine that's where I am. Not sure of what direction I want things to take in the future. But to borrow a figure of speech from you, I think I should have some idea before the terrible winds of November set upon us." She turned and took his hands in hers. "But this is all very solemn, don't you think? After all, we don't have to decide everything today. We can set some of this aside and enjoy our time together." She pushed out her lower lip. "There, don't look so disappointed. We can change these notes to something less tragic. Bring back an idea from before. Seize the day."

He recalled having said before that she had the makings of a philosopher, but in this moment it seemed that she was more of a user of philosophy. Sometimes she used ideas as a way of venturing out, and sometimes she used them as a refuge. Today she seemed to be doing both, and it gave him a feeling of dissatisfaction. He would rather she just told him what she thought she might do, even if it left him out. But lacking that kind of definiteness, he was not going to pass up this day. So he took her in his arms under the open sky and drew her close.

Tobacco smoke hung in the air of the bunkhouse, mixed with the aroma of fried bacon. Rand Sullivan scraped at the bowl of his pipe, tapped it in the sardine can, and set the pipe on the table. After closing his knife and putting it away, he looked in the direction of Foster and Merriman.

"Al and Fred, you can go out on your usual rounds." The boss shifted. "Paul and George, I want the two of you to work with El today, right here at the place. You know where that old root cellar is. Well, I want you to cave it in. It's startin' to sag, and I don't want the kids to get hurt playin' on top of it or inside of it."

Beckwith raised his head, and his close-set eyes had a calm expression. "Just knock it in?"

"No," said the boss. "Take the roof down first. Some of the wood is rotten, so be careful. Save anything that's good enough for stove wood, and bury the rest. Fill in the whole thing so it's level with the ground. That means you'll have to move the dirt that they mounded up when they first dug the thing. However long ago that was. I'd say at least twenty years."

Beckwith took a drag on his cigarette and blew the smoke to one side. "Sure. Movin' the dirt is likely to take a while, but we can get it done."

The boss gave a short smile. "I know you can. That's why I picked the best men for the job." He looked around the table. "You boys know where the tools are. Just be careful. All that dirt on the roof is heavy, and then there'll be rusty nails. Don't anyone step on one, for Pete's sake."

Elwood nodded. Crandall sniffed, and Beckwith said, "You bet." Foster and Merriman sat back from the table, each one with a boot hiked up on a knee, smoke drifting upward from their cigarettes.

"Well, that's good for now," said the boss. He stood up, holding his pipe by the bowl. He tucked it into his vest pocket, put on his hat, and left the bunkhouse.

Beckwith took a last drag on his cigarette and stubbed it out. "Might as well get goin'," he said.

Crandall stayed seated with his boot on the rung of his chair. "I'm not lookin' forward to this job."

Beckwith stood up. "Looks like just the thought of it has you broke out in a sweat. But it won't kill you. If you're careful."

Elwood rose from his chair, took his hat from the peg, and went outside to wait for the other two. Rand Sullivan was going up the steps to the ranch house. Past the house, a few yards to the right of the corral, sat the root cellar that they were supposed to fill in.

Foster and Merriman walked past Elwood with the air of two schoolboys who were getting off easy. They headed toward the barn and their day's work of riding.

Crandall and Beckwith stepped out of the bunkhouse, and as they strolled up to Elwood, Crandall mimicked the boss's words. "You boys know where the tools are."

The three of them walked to the barn. In a dark corner, Elwood sorted out the tools they would need—a pick, a digging bar, and three shovels. He handed them to Beckwith, who handed them all to Crandall and said, "I'll go find a hammer and a crowbar."

Elwood stepped back from the dark corner, took the three shovels, and led the way out of the barn. He waited at the front of the root cellar as Crandall poked along with the pick and the digging bar. A minute later, Beckwith showed up with a crowbar, a claw hammer, and a hand sledge.

After the three of them took turns peeking inside, Beckwith sent Crandall for a rope so they could pull out the support posts. Beckwith stooped and went inside to tie the rope on the post in back. As he led the rope out, he said, "We'll yank these king posts out one by one."

Crandall gave his low laugh. "I like queen posts better."

"Well, there aren't any of those here. Hang onto this rope."

Elwood hoped that the whole thing would come down at once, but instead it sagged and spilled and leaned until they pulled out the front post. Then the closer half of the roof came down with a *whoosh*, and a cloud of dust filled the void.

"I don't like any of this," said Crandall as he stood back with his hands on his hips.

Beckwith coiled the rope and pulled the post toward him. "Just loosen that loop, and don't step on any nails."

They worked on through the morning, knocking apart the lumber and the slender logs and tossing aside the salvaged wood. It was dirty work, with the constant rising and spilling of the fine, sifted dust that had accumulated over the years. The powdery dust and the cobwebs and the decayed wood combined to make a musty, unhealthy smell. Elwood wrinkled his nose and worked on.

When the men had the demolition complete, they began loosening the mounded dirt and throwing it onto the depression. Crandall had a stream of complaints, and every ten minutes he would take off his gloves and look for blisters. Beckwith, in contrast, seemed to be pleased at being the lead man in the day's work. At noontime he gave the word to knock off for dinner.

As the three men washed up at the pump, Crandall took off his hat and fanned himself. "I'll tell you," he said, "after we finish this job, I don't care if I ever see another shovel."

Beckwith wiped the excess water from his face and blew a breath of air to complete the process. "Damn few men in this kind of work are goin' to get by without usin' a shovel or a pitchfork. Fewer all the time. Isn't that right, El?"

Elwood opened his eyes. He had been left out of the conversation so much that he was surprised at being included. "I'd go along with that," he said.

"As for not seein' a shovel," Beckwith went on, "just be glad you can. There comes a time when they throw dirt in your face, and you'll never see anything again, not even the shovel they're usin'."

"I can tell this work has cheered you up." Crandall put on his hat and pushed at the turned-up brim.

Beckwith put on his own black and dusty hat. "Just glad I wasn't at the bottom of that heap. Whoever built that thing is prob'ly dead and gone. Work like this makes you glad to be above ground. That right, El?"

"Sure does." Then to himself, *It brings out the philosopher.* Elwood splashed water on his face, rubbed his eyes, and rinsed. He was tired and sweating, but he had no complaints. If he had wished for anything, it would have been for a glimpse of a dress and a parasol, but no one had come out of the ranch house all morning.

Elwood rested his horse on a knoll as he watched a buggy roll along the road that led to the ranch. He had not seen Josephine for two days, and he was on the lookout for anything that might be related to her withdrawal. The man who was driving the buggy stopped and waved to him, so he rode down the hill and brought his horse alongside the vehicle.

The man holding the reins looked as if he had come from somewhere else. He wore a brown derby hat and a brown suit, and his skin did not have the dry texture of people who lived on the high plains. He had a full mustache and one eyelid that was beginning to droop, and he filled out his vest. Elwood noted that he held a cigar between two fingers. People in grass country, as a general rule, did not smoke on the rangeland unless they were sitting still.

"Good afternoon," said the stranger. "Is this the road to the Crown Butte Ranch?"

"It sure is. Follow it for another five miles or so, and it'll take you right into the ranch."

"Thanks." The man lifted his cigar and took a puff. "Nice weather."

"Yes, it is." Elwood noted the bay horse in harness. Its black mane and reddish-brown coat glistened in the sunlight.

"Good for you and your work, I hope."

"If I'm not gettin' hailed or rained on, it's good for me. At this time of year, at least."

"Well, that's good. Actually, it's a bit warm." The man lifted his hat to let the air cool his head. His hair was thin on top and beaded with sweat. "Five miles, you say?"

"Yes, sir. About that."

The man settled his hat on his head and snugged it. "So long, then."

"We'll see you later."

The buggy was sitting in front of the ranch house when Elwood rode in at the end of the day. The bay horse that had drawn the vehicle stood in a pen by itself, dozing on its feet.

Nothing had changed by morning, but the buggy was gone when Elwood came in at midday. Otis confirmed that the man had come to visit Josephine.

"He seems to have a purpose about him," Otis said.

"Then he probably didn't go back to where he came from."

"No. From what I understand, he's staying in town."

Elwood did not see Josephine when he went out to saddle a horse for the afternoon, nor did he see her in the later afternoon when he came in. He made himself available after supper, lingering around the barn and the buckboard, and all he got for his trouble was unresolved anxiety, plus a few mosquito bites. Time and again he recalled her words and the light laugh that went with them. *A period of indecision.*

He still did not see her for the next two days. As far as he knew, the man in the derby hat did not visit the ranch in that time, either. It was now Saturday, and the other bunkhouse hands were planning to go to town. Elwood decided to go along, but Otis said he would stay at the ranch.

In a lowered voice, Elwood said, "Maybe you could help me with something."

"What's that?"

"Do you know the name of the fellow who came out here in the buggy?"

"Burgess," said Otis. "Richard Burgess."

Elwood saddled the palomino to go to town. The horse's coat was at its darkest in the summer, a deep golden color in contrast with the whitish mane and tail. Elwood thought he would cut a good figure as he rode out of the ranch in the dusk, but he felt a sad, almost hopeless feeling as he wondered whether she would even look out the window.

All the way into town he felt as if he was tied up in knots, and the first mug of beer did not loosen him. With the second one, he began to relax, but he found himself searching the crowd for Richard Burgess. He told himself that his searching was about as productive as hoping to find a lost letter from Josephine out on the rangeland.

A hand on his shoulder brought him back to the moment. He turned and met the sagging, dissolute features of Angell Gunn.

The man forced a smile and said, "Oh, it's you. I thought you were someone else, standing here all alone. But I remember you. We met in here, when? A couple, three weeks ago." He stuck out his hand. "Angell Gunn."

"Elwood." They shook.

"I remember your name." Angell Gunn smiled. "Do you always drink alone?"

"No. I came in with some other fellas. I'll join 'em in a little while."

"That's good. This is the time of life to have fun. When you're young."

"Wouldn't miss out on it."

"Not that an old tomcat can't cut the mustard. Ha-ha-ha-ha-ha." When the laugh ended, he spoke in an almost confidential tone. "Seemed to me you were lookin' for someone."

"Nah. Just gazin'. The product of an absent mind."

Angell Gunn clapped him on the shoulder again. "Ha-ha. My mind went absent a long time ago. Never came back. Well, so long, young feller. We'll see you again."

"You bet." As Angell Gunn moved along, Elwood realized he had been looking for someone else in addition to Richard Burgess, or at least expecting to see him. But the man in the dark hat and stovepipe boots was as absent as Lily of the West.

According to Otis, the buggy came and went on Monday while Elwood was out on the range, and Mrs. Newton was still in the ranch house. Along with the undercurrent of anxiety that did not go away, Elwood felt there was something irrational, almost absurd, in her being that close and knowing how he felt, yet staying in her tower, as it were, and letting him wait. For as much as she had studied the ways of the country and knew the value that was placed on straight dealing, here she was, acting like a stranger.

But as Rand Sullivan said before, they had other things to think about. Beckwith and Crandall had not come back to the ranch since the five of them had gone to town on Saturday night. They had gone off on their own, as they often did, but they did not show up at the bunkhouse on Sunday or Monday. When Elwood got up on Tuesday morning, their bunks were still empty. On Tuesday evening, Rand Sullivan had news.

He came to the bunkhouse as the men were finishing supper. He did not take off his hat or sit down, and he did not have his usual calm air. "I got a message about Paul and George this afternoon," he said. "They got into some trouble over in Hartville, and they're in the jail there."

"Hartville?" said Otis.

Sullivan's mouth was making tight motions. "That's right. I don't know what they were doing way the hell over there, or why they got put in jail, but I've got to go there and pick up those horses or I'll have a feed bill I can't pay. You know how they are in that place."

The men around the table nodded. Elwood had been through the town only once, and his visit confirmed the general reputation Hartville had of being a rough town, unfriendly to outsiders. It was forty miles away to the west and south, a long ride, but it was the kind of place where Beckwith and Crandall could meet with birds of their feather. It was also a good place to get thrown in jail.

The boss took a loud breath through his nose. "I've just about had it with those two. Now this. As if I didn't have anything else to do. Otis, I'm askin' you to pack their gear. El, you can go with me. We'll take their stuff and leave it there, along with their wages. We'll bring the two horses back. Make sure we've got ropes to lead 'em with."

"Leave first thing in the morning?"

"Yeah." The boss sounded weary. "I got this news too late in the day to do anything sooner. I had to think it through, take out some maps and look at 'em. Looks like there's a couple of ways to go."

Elwood said, "I traveled up from there one time. Went through a range called the Haystack Hills or the Haystack Buttes. Rough country for a wagon but not all that bad on horseback. No tellin' if the other way is easier."

"Your way is shorter on the map, so we'll try that. Looks like a full day's ride."

"It's all of that, but we can do it. I'll be ready at daybreak."

Elwood and Sullivan rode into Hartville at about nine on Thursday morning, having decided to camp on the trail overnight and take care of business in the light of day.

The town had not changed since Elwood had seen it before. It was pitched in a gulch, uphill from the Platte Valley to the south and the grasslands to the north, yet surrounded by higher hills. Red dust from a nearby iron mine lay on the road, on wagons, on horses, and on the clothes of some of the people who paused and watched them as they rode in.

Elwood waited outside the jail and held the horses while Sullivan went in. The boss came out ten minutes later, followed by a lanky young man with fuzzy red hair and no hat. Elwood continued to hold the horses as Sullivan untied the two bundles, heaped both of them onto the spindly outstretched arms of the young man, and followed him back inside. A couple of minutes later, the boss came out with a light step.

"Two blocks down to the stable," he said as he took his reins.

Sullivan paid the stableman and led the two bare horses, both sorrels, out into the sunlight. Elwood put a neck rope onto each one, and Sullivan took the halters back into the stable.

When he came out he said, "Those boys will be on foot, but at least they'll have their saddles and their other gear all in one place. What they do or where they go is up to them."

"Would it be out of place to ask what they got thrown in for?"

The boss looked straight at Elwood, and with a shake of the head he said, "Barroom stuff. So their wages'll be enough to get 'em out. I wish they'd been caught for somethin' else, or that I'd been able to get somethin' on 'em, but at least I'm done with 'em. I hope so, anyway." He heaved a breath as he put his foot in the stirrup and pulled himself aboard.

Elwood handed him the rope to one of the sorrels. Holding the other rope clear, he mounted the dark horse and fell into line alongside the boss. They rode east toward the trail that would take them past the iron mine again, back through the Haystack Buttes, and on to their home range. The sun was high enough that Elwood could shade it out by tipping his hat forward and tucking his head.

Dust rose in the street along with the clopping sound of four sets of horse hooves. Elwood sat relaxed in the saddle, swaying with the movement of the dark horse and trying not to seem concerned about any strangers who might be watching them.

The sound of Sullivan clearing his throat made Elwood look up and around. On the left side of the street, standing on the board sidewalk in the shade of an overhang, stood two men whose features were familiar. The man in the black hat, black vest, and stovepipe boots was taller than the other. Although Elwood could not pick out the shorter man's blue eyes, he could see the contrast between his pink nose and muddy complexion.

At the edge of town, Elwood spoke just loud enough for Sullivan to hear him. "Armitage and Driggs. I wonder how much of a coincidence it is that they're here."

"No tellin'. But that's what their boss gets for not mindin' the store. Fella like him, comes from back east, wants to make easy money with no effort. Expects free grass, free water, free firewood, and cheap labor, not to mention any free cows he can get his hands on. So if his hired men are out pullin' somethin', I don't feel sorry for him."

Elwood rode on in thought. After a minute he said, "Sometimes I think about Driggs's old partner, Haden, and where he is. I wonder if he's workin' for Jennings, too."

"I wouldn't be surprised. You know the old saying. There's always one more son of a bitch than you counted on."

Chapter Ten

Elwood rotated his whiskey glass on the table in front of him. Across the table, Foster and Merriman were smoking cigarettes and tapping to the piano music. To his right, Otis was craning his neck to see who sat at the other tables and stood along the bar of the Northern Star Saloon.

Elwood was intent on seeing only one person, Richard Burgess, and that was only to know if the man was still in town. Elwood understood from Otis that Burgess had come to the ranch once while he and Sullivan went on the trip to Hartville. Otis said he had no impression as to whether anything definite had taken place, and Elwood was left to guess whether the silence from within the ranch house came from embarrassment, guilt, indecision, or some cause he was yet to understand. And the irony was not lost upon him that he had to travel nearly fifteen miles to town to see if he could find a clue to a puzzle wrapped in silence some fifty yards away.

"No sign of a fellow in a derby hat?" he asked as Otis settled back into his chair.

Otis shook his head. "I don't know if he'd come in here, but it's the main place to while away a little time. All the dignitaries of the cowpunchin' trade, not to mention sheepherders, railroad graders, and freighters—well, there's someone now."

Elwood followed Otis's line of sight to the front door, where a man dressed in black had made his appearance and was looking over the crowd. Elwood said, "I told you I saw him in Hartville."

"Uh-huh. He must get around."

"Him and Driggs. Come to think of it, I haven't seen the two of them together here in town. Just when they're out and about, tending to some kind of business."

"And who knows what kind."

Elwood went back to studying his drink while out of the corner of his eye he saw Armitage walk up to the bar and tap a silver dollar, edge up, on the varnished top.

A small commotion rose from down the bar a ways. A group of cowpunchers was laughing and shouting and pushing one man towards the middle of the floor where the piano sat.

"It's the Four Bills," said Otis.

"Oh." Elwood raised his head to look their way. He recognized the four men who were all named Bill. Two of them were Jigger-Y waddies, and two of them rode for other outfits. When they got together, they liked to make a show of good humor.

Right now, they were pushing one of their foursome out to sing alone with the piano player. The other three began stomping their feet, clapping, and chanting, "Go, Bill. Go, Bill."

The piano player had stopped. He sat with his eyes upraised at Bill, who stood as if he were on an island. He took a couple of steps forward, exchanged some words with the piano player, and stood straight up with his shoulders squared. A familiar tune came out of the piano, and Bill began to sing in a loud, measured voice.

De Camptown ladies come to town,
doo-da, doo-da.
De Camptown ladies sing this song,
doo-da, doo-da, day.
'Gwine to run all night, 'gwine to run all day,

I bet my money on the bob-tail nag,
Somebody bet on the bay.

Some of the other patrons had joined in and were whooping it up along with the other three Bills. Bill the singer looked aside at them, nodded, and went into his next verse.

De Camptown races come to town,
doo-da, doo-da.
De Camptown racetrack two miles long,
doo-da, doo-da, day.
'Gwine to run all night, 'gwine to run all day,
I bet my money on the bob-tail nag,
Somebody bet on the bay.

Foster and Merriman were clapping, and Otis was singing along.

'Gwine to run all night, 'gwine to run all day,
I bet my money on the bob-tail nag,
Somebody bet on the bay.

Elwood let his gaze drift toward the bar. Armitage stood with his back to the crowd, watching in the mirror. Something caused him to perk up, take his elbow from the bar, and draw himself to his full height. After a few seconds he turned and with casual regard gave the appearance of seeing for the first time a chunky man in a brown suit and brown derby hat.

"Ah-hah," said Otis. "What do you think they have in common?"

"I'd say they both came from somewhere else."

Otis nodded his head. "I think that fits. They're both strangers, just two different kinds."

The piano music stopped, and applause was mixed with

whoops and hollers. Bill made a motion of returning to his group at the bar, but the insistence of the crowd kept him on the floor. He spoke to the piano player, and they launched into another familiar song.

When I was young I used to wait
And meet my master at the gate,
Pass the bottle when he got dry,
And brush away the blue-tail fly.

The tempo picked up with the fourth line and then the chorus, which some of the patrons sang along with Bill.

Elwood glanced at the bar again. Armitage and Burgess were conversing in a matter-of-fact way.

Bill sang only two stanzas about the blue-tail fly, and after the horse had pitched the mater in the ditch, he went through the chorus twice and took off his hat and raised it. More cheers and jeers came from the crowd, but Bill shook his head.

"I'd sing more," he said, "but I don't know any. Leastwise, I can't remember 'em right now."

As Bill walked back to the bar amid calls of "Aw, c'mon, Bill," and "Just one more," the piano player broke into the tune of "Sweet Betsy from Pike" and began singing in a voice that was not very loud.

Elwood, having heard many versions of the song, thought this one could go on for a long time, but the piano player sang only six stanzas or so and finished when the Shanghai rooster ran off, the cattle all died, and the dog looked wondrously sad.

Motion at the bar caught Elwood's eye. Burgess pushed his empty glass away, squared up, and shook Armitage's hand. Paying no attention to anyone else in the saloon, he walked out.

Armitage also ignored the crowd by keeping his back to everyone, though Elwood caught his beady eyes in the mirror a couple of times. A few minutes after Burgess left, Armitage did the same.

The boys from the Crown Butte Ranch sat in peace at their table. Otis rolled a tight pill for himself. A few minutes later, Foster and Merriman rolled cigarettes and smoked in their calm, unhurried way. The man at the piano had gone back to playing and not singing. The songs were slow, three-beat melodies that drifted in and out of Elwood's awareness as he thought about the noncommittal silence of Josephine, the continued presence of Burgess, and the unexpected acquaintance of Burgess and Armitage. Yet it all made sense. Whether her making it up to him was planned as a limited-term affair or whether it turned out that way because of Burgess's arrival and perseverance, Elwood could see that the end of the story was not going to be a happy one—at least for him, which was all he could make himself care about at the moment.

"Uh-oh," said Otis. "Here comes a pair."

Elwood came out of his daze and saw Crandall and Beckwith walking toward the Crown Butte table. They hadn't lost much time getting back to town, and they didn't look any different. Crandall wore his gray hat turned up in front, his red neckerchief not recently laundered, his collarless gray shirt, and his dark-gray canvas vest. He was smiling, and his yellow teeth were visible. Beckwith wore his dusty black hat, charcoal-gray vest, and striped gray cotton shirt. His dark stubble was four or five days along, and his dark, close-set eyes shifted as they often did.

They came to a stop at the Crown Butte table, Crandall a little ahead of Beckwith and close enough that Elwood could see the yellow crust on his teeth.

"Hullo, boys." Crandall put his thumbs in his belt.

Everyone at the table returned the greeting.

"You got back pretty quick," said Otis.

Crandall, still smiling, said, "Nothin' serious to keep us there.

It would've been easier to ride the same horses back, but we made it." He looked at Elwood. "No hard feelin's, of course. I suppose the old man's put out at us, but I don't blame him." Crandall looked over his shoulder. "Huh, Paul?"

"Oh, yeah." Beckwith did not smile, but his face relaxed.

Crandall stretched as he scratched the back of his neck. "We'll find another job. We always do. Everyone does. Meanwhile, it's good to see you boys."

"You bet," said Otis. "And good luck."

Crandall said, "Thanks," and Beckwith nodded.

As the two of them walked to the bar, Elwood widened his eyes and looked at the other three. Foster and Merriman each shrugged, and Otis said, "Well, that's one way to save face. Not bad, as far as it goes."

The murmur of the crowd blended again with the notes of the piano. Elwood drifted in his thoughts until Otis spoke his name.

"El."

"Huh?"

Otis motioned with his head toward a man who stood at Elwood's left.

The man said, "I understand your name's Elwood."

"It is."

"My name's Rudd Robinett. Do you have a minute?"

Elwood gave the man a once-over. His first thought was that Robinett might be a detective or something in that line. He was dressed in a lightweight, light-colored, bluish-gray suit with a matching vest, and he wore a short-brimmed, creased hat of a similar color. His white shirt had a starched collar snugged with a short gray necktie, and a watch chain drooped from his vest pocket. He was of average height and build, with blue eyes, brown hair, and a trimmed mustache. His mouth looked a little crooked, perhaps because of the way he set it in an expression of firmness.

"I guess so," said Elwood. "Would you like to sit here?"

"If you don't mind." The stranger pulled a chair from the next table and sat next to Elwood. Leaning so he would not have to speak so loud, he said, "This is all on the square, so don't worry."

Elwood nodded and took a sip of whiskey. "Care for a drink?"

"Not right now, thanks. But I'd be glad to buy you one."

"I'm fine. We've got a bottle for the table."

"I see." Robinett made a small noise of clearing his throat, and fixing his blue eyes on Elwood, he said, "I understand you knew a man named D. W. Stanley."

"Only in passing."

"I understand you knew him better than anyone else and asked around about him."

"Not much."

"Oh. Didn't mean to seem too forward. This is just what I was told. I was sorry to hear what happened to him."

"Did you know him?"

Robinett shook his head. "No. But I'm interested in talking about what he might have told you."

"I don't know anything more than the next fellow. He stayed one night at the ranch, and he sat down for a while at our table in here, just like you're doin', except he had a drink."

"He must have had interesting conversation. They say he was a likeable sort."

"Anyone could tell you the same."

"I see. In other words, you don't care to discuss it much further."

"I wouldn't contradict you on that."

"No harm done." Robinett pushed back his chair and stood up. He put on a smile as he held out his hand. "Thanks all the same. Maybe we'll get to talk again."

"Pleased to meet you."

Robinett took out his watch with an air of authority, opened it, and gave it an appraising look. He clicked it shut, and as he walked away he slipped it back into his vest pocket.

Otis leaned toward Elwood and said, "What's he up to?"

"Said he wanted to ask me about that traveler named Stanley who died here. I don't know what his game is, but I didn't trust him." Elwood watched the man make his way to the bar. "If he knew enough to ask me, he would have known just about anything I did." Elwood shrugged. "I just didn't like the feel of it."

Elwood kept his eye on the bar. Robinett found a place and rested his forearm on the bar top. He spoke to Ned the bartender, and a moment later he had a drink in front of him. He didn't touch it for a couple of minutes, and when he did, he paused before lifting it. His attention was taken by a man at his left, a man in a concho hatband and a linen duster.

Angell Gunn spoke and waited for an answer. He tipped his head back, leaned forward, spoke again, and shook hands. He talked a little more, pointed at Robinett, and broke into his artificial laugh that carried to the Crown Butte table.

"That's Angell Gunn," said Elwood. "The one I told you about."

Otis gave a close look. "Oh, yeah."

Angell Gunn spoke again, and Robinett was a picture of attention. Angell Gunn rocked back and forth, pointed his hand like a gun, and poked Robinett in the ribs. Then he opened his mouth and let out his automatic laugh. Robinett continued to pay attention with a straight face.

"Who knows what they're talkin' about," said Elwood. "But there's a man who'll give him plenty to listen to."

Quint was standing in the hot sun wearing his short-brimmed

hat and beating a stick on the mound of dirt where the root cellar used to be. To Elwood it seemed like a normal activity for a six-year-old, and he was glad the little boy's father had decided to cave in the cellar.

Elwood walked up at a casual pace and called out, "Hello, Quint."

The boy paused with his stick and looked around, squinting. "Hi, El."

"Gettin' in a few licks?"

"Just hittin' it."

"That's good. Say, do you think you could take in a note for me? For Mrs. Newton?"

"You mean Josie?"

"That's right. Same person. Nothing secret about it. I just don't want to go to the door and trouble anyone myself."

"Now?"

"If you're not too busy."

The boy looked at the dirt where the end of his stick was resting. "I guess not."

Elwood took the note out of his shirt pocket, unfolded it, and read it one last time.

Dear Josie:

I was wondering if you might have a few minutes to talk. I won't take much of your time.

Yours,

El

He folded the paper and handed it to the boy. "Thanks, Quint," he said. "I'll be around in case there's any message back."

"Okay." Quint pulled at the stick, held it straight up like a staff, and marched to the house.

Elwood walked past the corrals and loitered in front of the

barn where he had met her on a couple of other occasions. The day being Sunday, he was free to spend it as he wished, so he felt entitled to stand around in the middle of the day. He brushed a fly from his sleeve, checked to see that his shirt was tucked in. He thought back to the moment, earlier in the day, when he had sat on the edge of his bunk and held the blue shirt he had bought in town shortly after roundup. He had not worn the shirt yet, and he had thought about it for a long moment. Now, as he stood in the sunlight in front of the barn and considered how easily he could be made to look and feel like a fool today, he was glad he had chosen not to wear the new shirt.

After about ten minutes he heard the door of the house open, and he turned to see Josephine walking down the steps.

She was wearing a gray dress with darker gray stripes and balancing a parasol on her shoulder. She had a serious expression on her face, suggesting pain or regret. He felt that whatever resurgence of hope had come with her return was gone now, and as she came close enough to speak, he sensed an invisible barrier, like a pane of glass, between them. She was untouchable.

"Good afternoon," she said, in a subdued but cordial tone.

"Good afternoon. I hope I don't seem impatient."

"Not at all. I know I've been putting you off. I've felt terrible about it, but there has never seemed to be the right moment for me to speak to you."

"My time's pretty open."

A pained expression came onto her face and disappeared. "What I mean is that I have wanted a moment at which I could say definitely what I was going to do and what it would mean for each of us. That is, I kept waiting for the moment to be right, and it never quite was."

"I don't think there's much point in my getting worked up about what hasn't happened."

"That's nice of you to say, but all the same, I'm sorry."

He shrugged. "Please don't feel that you have to apologize."

"Thank you."

Up until this moment he had not looked straight at her, but now he did. Her eyes were an indistinct color between light brown and green, and her face was paler than he remembered. He took a full breath and said, "I suppose I'm like anyone else. I just want to know where I stand."

She looked down. "I know that, and I feel perfectly miserable for having been so indecisive."

"We've been pretty close," he said. "We've been able to say some, I don't know, ground-level things to one another. Not rock-bottom, maybe, but—"

"Fundamental. Basic."

"That's what I mean. So I don't see any reason why we can't be straight with one another at this point."

"You're right. Of course you're right. But—"

"But what?"

"I don't know what to say—that is, I don't know what there is to say, much less how to say it. I'm not like you. I can't reduce things to their size and weight and—duration, or length of life."

"Do I do that?"

"You know things. How much a steer weighs, how hot or cold it gets at a certain time, when the snakes come out, when the bad winds blow."

"I'd better know something, or I won't last long in this country."

"Well, I try to know things, too, but it's not the same. So it's hard to know what to say."

"Maybe I could help."

She gave him a look that expressed reservation. "In what way?"

"I could ask you a question or two."

"I don't know. I might not have an answer, depending on the question. But go ahead."

He had prepared his question well ahead of time. "Are you choosing this other fellow? Note that I'm not asking whether you're choosing him over me, just whether you're choosing him."

She hesitated for half a minute and said, "Well, yes, I guess I am." Then, in a tone suggesting that her statement was also prepared, she said, "I'm going to give a chance at sharing prospects with him."

It did not hit him as hard as he had expected, and he did not flinch at asking his next question. "Is he the one who provided the resources, as I think you put it, to knock your husband out of the picture?"

She gave an intake of breath. "He was very helpful. I don't think I could have done it on my own—in fact, I'm sure I couldn't have—if he hadn't helped me. He shored me up, talked sense into me when I wavered."

Elwood noted that she did not mention the financial aspect. He remembered well enough that he, too, had offered that kind of help, and he was sure she had not forgotten it. But he tried to answer in the terms she had used. "So now you follow the path of least resistance. You're in debt to this fellow in one way or another, and he pushes for what he wants."

"You could put it that way."

He thought he detected a note of resentment in her comment, but he was not out to try to win her back. That cause was lost, he was sure, and all he had left was the chance to tell her what he thought. "He's no good for you, Josie. He uses money and leverage to get what he wants, and sooner or later you'll regret it."

"I don't know that yet."

"I just don't think he's a square dealer. He's not good for

you. For all I know, he may be crooked in other ways, but in this thing, I can tell. I'm no expert, and I'm no philosopher, but when it comes to things between a woman and a man, it's not good when somebody wants to win or wants to have things his way."

She looked at him now, and she seemed farther away than ever before. She said, "I can't refute that, but I've already agreed."

"To go with him."

"Yes."

He felt as if a wall of bricks fell to the ground at his feet, but at the same time his anger rose within him. "Then what perfect moment could you have been waiting for to tell me?"

She shook her head. "I don't know."

He let out a long breath, and his anger faded with it. "Then I guess we don't have much more to talk about."

"No," she said, "except perhaps to say that I don't regret anything except the way I've made you suffer."

That, too, seemed like a rehearsed line, but he didn't mind it. "It's all right, Josie. Like I said before, I don't hurt that easy. I just wonder if I would have done anything different if I had known our last time together was the last."

"I'm glad I didn't," she said. Then she laughed. "I could have ruined it for both of us." She held out her hands. "In case I don't get a chance to say it later, I'll say it now. Thank you for everything, and I wish you the best."

"So long. And the same to you." In his heart he knew he did not wish her the best, not with her new champion, at least, but in saying as little as he did, he did not lie. That was a small comfort, but he took it.

Elwood went back to the bunkhouse, feeling detached from the world. His senses swam. He could see and hear perfectly, but he felt as if his feet didn't quite touch the ground and his hands couldn't quite reach what was in front of him. Yet he turned the handle on the door and went in.

Foster and Merriman were seated at the table playing checkers. Their voices blended to say, "Hello, El." Otis looked up from reading a spread-out newspaper to say the same.

"Hello," he answered, and he could hear the fatigue in his own voice. He hung his hat and went to his bunk, where he stretched out with his hands clasped behind his head. That was the way things went, he told himself. A woman leaves her husband and finds someone to help her in a physical and emotional way. Then she goes back, and she leaves her husband again, this time finding someone to help her in a financial and authoritative kind of way. Elwood heaved a sigh. The sequence was probably not that simple. If he had come back into the story after Burgess had helped demolish the husband, it was likely that Burgess had been in the story when she came to the ranch the first time. But regardless of when he came into the game, Burgess had plenty at stake. Maybe he was a little pudgy and looked out of place in his city clothes, but he could get things done. And if his way was what it took to win a woman like Josephine—well, that was the way things went. She had chosen the other man.

He was just going to have to accept that. He could accept it now, as an idea, but he could feel himself still fighting it off, as he had done when he knew his cause was lost and he argued on anyway.

He opened his hands and closed them. He felt restless all through his body. With a tightening of his stomach muscles he sat up, then swung around and sat on the edge of his bunk. He needed to do something.

If there was anything to be thankful for at the moment, it was that Crandall and Beckwith weren't around to irritate him. Foster and Merriman kept to their game of checkers as he crossed the room and picked his hat off the peg. He went to the back door and took the ax by the end of the handle.

Otis looked up from his newspaper. "What are you doing?"

"I think I'll chop some wood."

"It's Sunday. I've got enough for now."

"I'm all on edge. I need something to do. Cutting up those old posts seems like just the thing."

"Suit yourself."

Elwood went out back and had at it. The first post was dry and hard, but he made the chips fly. Little chips. He was in no hurry. He cut the post through once, again, and again. His arms were tired and he was breathing hard as he put the four pieces in a little stack. He stood up straight for a couple of minutes with his hand on the tip of the ax handle as he took a breather. Then he went after the next post.

He had finished all three posts and was sitting on the back step, gazing at the stack of a dozen stove lengths, when movement caught his eye. A buggy was coming along the road to the ranch. He recognized the bay horse, the canopy, and the man in the derby hat. The buggy rolled into the yard and past his line of vision.

He went inside and put the ax away. After drinking two tall glasses of water, he carried in the new firewood. He sat on the edge of his bunk for a few minutes, deciding what to do next. No, he told himself. Even if it meant giving himself pain, he wasn't going to sit inside and keep from seeing it.

He got up, put on his hat, and went out the back door. He walked around the end of the bunkhouse farthest from the barn and ranch house, and his timing could not have been better. Voices made him stop. He had a clear view, and no one looked his way.

Josephine stood on the walkway in front of the house and facing it. Her parasol, not yet opened, lay on her shoulder as she spoke to Mrs. Sullivan, who stood on the top step shading her eyes. Burgess was carrying two large traveling bags toward the buggy. Even at a distance he exuded an air of authority and purpose as he swung one bag and then the other into the back of the buggy.

The voices rose in a tone of farewell. Mrs. Sullivan waved a handkerchief as Josephine turned and walked toward the buggy. She held the folded parasol forward like a sword as Burgess handed her up and into the carriage. She settled onto her seat, opened the parasol, and held it at the edge of the canopy. Burgess walked around and hauled himself into the driver's seat, and after saying something to Josephine he put the buggy into motion. Voices called out as the bay horse made a half circle, and the parasol blocked Josephine from Elwood's view as the buggy rolled away.

Elwood let out a heavy breath. There had been a little pain, like pushing against a sore tooth, but he was glad he had made himself endure it. He recalled the tooth that Crandall carried around with him. Maybe someday he, Elwood, could look at this thing as if it were an object in his hand, but first it was going to have to settle in so he could worry it some more.

Chapter Eleven

Elwood let the speckled horse move at its own pace across the open grassland. Each of the horses in his string knew the trail he followed when he left the ranch and went to scout the range to the west and northwest. As the pale horse traveled at a fast walk, Elwood surveyed the country around him.

The land was the same as always, but like the rest of his world in the past few days, it seemed detached, as if there were some invisible shell or bubble that moved with him. He could not remember a time when he did not know what glass was, but he had heard of children who grew up in the country and had never seen glass. To explain what it was, an older person would hold up a sheet of ice from a water trough. If the ice was transparent, the older person would explain that glass was similar. For his own interest, Elwood had held up a sheet of ice on a couple of occasions and looked through. It had a blur to it, something like water, and it made things on the other side seem out of reach, but it still resembled glass if only for a while.

That was the sensation he had now. Though he could see the grass and sagebrush, mouse holes and anthills, and even the bugs themselves with perfect clarity, it was as if a watery pane separated him from the world.

He rode on, seeing the things of the world around him but not taking them in. So it was with a wisp of dry grass hanging in midair about a foot above the trail. It disappeared as the horse walked forward. Still in something of a daze, Elwood stared downward, past the gray mane and speckled front of the horse, and saw the string. It moved as the horse's ankle pushed against it.

A jolt of realization went through him and he yanked on the reins, but it was too late. The horse flinched, spooked, and bolted. A rustling, thrashing sound came from the sagebrush, followed a split second later by the blast of a gun. Dust and bits of sagebrush filled the air as the horse bucked and kicked and broke into a dead run. The shotgun bounced at the end of the string and dragged in the dirt, then disappeared from Elwood's sight as it dropped behind.

Elwood hung on and got the horse stopped within fifty yards. He dismounted and tried to look at its hindquarters, but the horse kept moving away. With a firm grip on the reins, Elwood reached back and grabbed the tail to make the animal stand still. Stretching out, he leaned further and saw a few nicks on the horse's lower back legs. Specks of red appeared, but no blood was flowing.

He walked the horse back toward the scene of the ambush. The shotgun lay in the middle of the trail with a length of twine still tied to the trigger guard. It had dirt in the barrel and along the ridge between the wooden forearm and the steel barrel. It was a single-shot, breakdown model, so it would have one expended shell in the breech. He picked up the gun, thumbed the lever, and ejected the casing just to make sure. He could see through the barrel to the dirt below.

He snapped the gun shut and held it at his side as he looked around at the countryside. Somebody had set this trap for him, someone who meant business. A person didn't have to be very bright to use dull-colored jute twine instead of cotton string, and even a stranger could have observed the route he followed whenever he rode out this way. Elwood imagined a devious person, cunning enough to know how to set a spring gun and clever enough to be miles away when it went off.

His first two candidates were George Crandall and Angell Gunn—Crandall with his coyote grin and his assurance of no hard feelings, and Angell Gunn with his bare-faced insistence that he wasn't following anyone.

Elwood took another look around. The pane of ice had melted, and everything was clear now, except the identity of who had set this trap. It was going to take some thinking.

He started with Crandall. He had assumed all along that Crandall and Beckwith had cut the cinch strap, and he didn't see any reason to think otherwise now. The incident had occurred when Elwood was out looking on a daily basis for signs of rustling. The act was malicious and could have caused injury, but it was petty in comparison with setting a shotgun.

Furthermore, this deadly trap was somewhat after the fact for Beckwith and Crandall to be setting it. Elwood had not found any real signs of misdoing since roundup, and by now the two punchers he thought were crooked were no longer in a position to do inside work and have to protect it.

That led him to Angell Gunn. Elwood had no doubt that the self-styled tough son of a bitch was following him that day, but he couldn't come up with a good reason why. Along the same line, he couldn't imagine why Angell Gunn would set a trap like this, even if he was capable, which he probably was.

Armitage and Driggs came to mind next. Even as Elwood summoned up their images he could feel their animosity, but again, he couldn't conceive of a reason strong enough for them to go out of their way to do something on this scale. Driggs had plenty of resentment, but he worked for Armitage, and as far as Elwood knew, Armitage didn't have any definite grudges against him.

His thought flickered for a moment, and he recalled the scene of Armitage and Burgess having a drink together. Now there was a possibility, but it was remote. Burgess had come, seen, and gotten what he wanted without giving any indication that a cowpuncher was worthy of his attention. For all Elwood knew, Josephine might not have even mentioned him to Burgess. He had a twinge of uneasiness as he remembered having told her that Burgess was no good for her and might be crooked in other ways, but in order for her to have passed that on, she would have had to let Burgess know that she had some level of confidence with a hired hand. Elwood made a dry smile. The odds were against it.

He wrapped up the whole bunch of men and counted them, including Haden so that there wouldn't be one more than he counted on. He came up with seven men, all of whom had some reason to dislike him but none of whom seemed to have enough reason to make this kind of move against him.

He opened the shotgun and looked down the barrel again to be sure it was empty. The day was warming up, and the smell of sage drifted on the air. The world was no longer out of whack, even if this act of treachery had him mystified. He had to keep thinking clearly. He clicked the gun shut and tied it to the saddle with the string below the swell on the left side.

Anyone else . . . any other strangers. Another image came to him, of a man trudging along the road from the southeast at the end of a warm day. D. W. Stanley. And the other man, the one who called himself Jim Farley. The second man disappeared, and the first one supposedly hanged himself. After that there was the straight-faced stranger named Robinett. Elwood shook his head. Stanley committing suicide hadn't made sense at the time, and it still didn't. Then there was the ticket to Omaha. Josephine had brushed it off as unimportant, and so had Ned the bartender.

Here was something to follow. A man had died in a questionable way, and he, Elwood, had asked about the man. His doing so was conspicuous enough for someone to mention it to Robinett. Probably Ned the bartender.

Elwood had to sort things into their proper order. When had he asked in town about Stanley? Before the cut strap, before he met Angell Gunn, before he saw Armitage and Driggs together.

Elwood used a leather lace to tie the barrel of the shotgun to the cinch ring so that the gun would not flop around.

Now for a backtrack. Stanley had died, and why? No one knew. Or maybe someone did. The lone traveler was the one person who seemed to know something about the man who disappeared. Elwood had asked about Stanley, and then Robinett had come asking after that.

Small things, some of them forgotten in the blooming and fading of romance and in following the cold trail of rustling. Nine men to keep track of, or ten, and four or five ways of grouping them. It was better to keep them sorted out.

Elwood pulled the knots tight where they held the shotgun in place. The twelve-gauge could be a little souvenir—not as dear as a tooth from his own mouth, but a reminder to keep a count on things. Before long he was going to have to go to town, and when he did, he would have to be careful about where he asked his questions.

The interior of the general store was dark and cool in comparison with the day outside, but as Elwood's eyes adjusted he could see the merchandise well enough. After the tinkling of the bell, the only sound was that of his boots on the wooden floor and the faint jingle of his spurs. Two-thirds of the way to the counter, he paused. Movement and sound came from somewhere up on the left. As he turned and looked upward, McDowell the storekeeper materialized at the top of the ladder that slid along the ledge. The man was dressed in light-colored clothes, including his apron, and he had his arms full of folded gray blankets. He looked down over his shoulder and gave a tense smile that barely showed his teeth.

"Be someone there in a minute," he said. He turned his head and called across his other shoulder. "Front!"

Footsteps sounded in the back of the store, and Sylvie Lamarre appeared in back of the counter. She was carrying a large pair of scissors with painted black handles. As she set them to one side on the counter, she smiled and spoke.

"Hello. What can I help you find today?"

"I thought I might take an interest in a couple of pairs of socks."

Her hair hung loose at her shoulders, and her dark eyes sparkled. "I can help you find them." She came around the counter, and her lavender-colored dress made a soft swishing sound. She led the way to the second aisle, the same one where she had helped him pick out the two shirts. As before, the smell of new clothing hovered about the stacks of trousers, overalls, and shirts. Then the dark and colored items gave way to shelves of pale undershirts, long underwear, and gray wool socks.

"These will do fine," he said as he picked up two pair near him.

"Not much deciding."

"I suppose I could linger a little more." He turned the socks over in his hands. He raised his eyes to meet hers, and without speaking very loud he said, "I'll tell you, I wasn't all that urgent to buy socks, but I could use a couple of pair. What I was wondering was, well, whether you have an interest in, or even have the liberty to—well, have a little time just for conversation."

"About something other than—?" She made a waving motion with her hand.

"Yes, about something other than merchandise. Although it's all very interesting." He waved at the clothing.

"Indeed. Wool, denim, canvas."

"Well, do you?"

She raised her chin. "Mr. Elwood, you have to understand that I'm a . . ."

His eyes widened, and his mouth opened. *Oh, no,* he thought.

She laughed. "You look so stricken."

He tried to smile as he searched her face for a hint. "I was afraid you were going to say—"

She shook her head as she broke into a full smile. "I'm sorry. It's just that you looked so—"

"Mortified?"

"I was going to say tortured, but that word will do. Anyway, yes, I could meet for conversation about something other than merchandise. The store doesn't close until seven today, but I could meet you then, rather than go back to my room first. That would put us too much later in the evening. How does that sound? I assume that today is good for you."

"Yes, it is. But I was prepared to come back some other time if I had to."

"You never know, but today is fine. It's the least I can do, after the scare I gave you."

He handed her the socks, and she led the way to the counter.

McDowell was there, with a vigilant air about him. "Find everything?"

"Oh, yes," said Sylvie.

"I'll handle this, then."

Sylvie laid the two pairs of socks on the counter, picked up the scissors, and headed for the back room.

"Wrap these?" asked McDowell.

Elwood decided to let him work for his profit. "That would be fine."

The storekeeper cut a piece of brown paper from the roll and made short work of wrapping the socks. His hands seemed to work by themselves as he pulled out a length of white string and snapped it with his thumbs and fists. "We've had good weather, haven't we?" He tied, rotated the package, and tied again. "There you are."

Elwood handed him a silver dollar. With a small bob of the head, the storekeeper opened the cash box and dipped out the change. "Everything's fine out at the ranch?"

"Seems to be."

McDowell showed his rabbit teeth. "Thank you so much," he said.

"And thanks to you." Elwood restrained himself from trying to catch another glimpse of Sylvie before he turned and walked out.

Sylvie was holding a small handbag and standing in the shade of the storefront when Elwood arrived for her at seven. She gave him an appraising look and said, "That's a nice shirt."

"Thanks. I had help picking it out. This is the first time I've worn it." He took off his hat. "Would you care to dine?"

"I suppose it wouldn't be a bad idea before we get too late."

"Dining room at the hotel?"

"That sounds agreeable."

They set out walking on the shady side of the street, and the scent of her perfume was pleasant. They walked the two blocks to the hotel, went in, and were seated without delay.

They ordered the evening meal, which consisted of fried chicken, cooked carrots, and rice.

"I hope you don't mind it," he said. "About the only time I eat chicken is in town. At the bunkhouse it's mostly beef, salt pork, or bacon."

"This is fine. Mrs. Wallace, where I stay, has chicken once in a while, but it seems that four days out of five she serves bacon gravy. The variation is whether she serves it over rice or potatoes." After a second she added, "Not that I complain."

"Oh, no. Me neither." As silence began to set in, he said, "So tell me about yourself. If you'd like to."

"Well, there's not much to tell. Doesn't seem like it. I'm originally from Montana, the youngest of five children in my family. As things worked out, it sort of fell to me to take care of my parents. My sisters were married, and my brothers were off on their own. So I didn't get out into the world, you might say, until just a few years ago. I've been a working girl, and I don't mind it. It's an honest living, and I get by all right." She took a drink from her water glass. "And yourself?"

"Pretty much as you've seen me. Hired hand. Cowpuncher and sometimes digger of postholes. Been at it for about fifteen years and expect to be good for a few more."

"Sounds like an honest living as well."

"I try to keep it that way." He met her eyes. "Can't say that everyone does, but that's a topic for somewhere else."

She nodded.

The meal came, and they made small talk, though little of it, as they ate. When they were done, he asked her if she would like to go on an evening stroll, and she agreed.

Out on the sidewalk, they walked past businesses that were closed for the night. He wasn't sure where to start in the conversation, but he went ahead and gave it a try.

"I would guess you've been in town long enough to know who some of the people are and what-all they do."

"I've gotten to know a few, but the person who knows the whole book is Mr. McDowell. He doesn't volunteer very much, but whenever I need to know something, I can get the story from him."

"I hope you don't mind if I ask your impressions of a couple of things. Of course I wouldn't want to put you in any kind of an uncomfortable position, so if there's anything you'd rather not answer—"

"Oh, don't worry. I'm not likely to get in much trouble that way. First off, I don't know much, and second, I don't talk over my head."

"Good enough." He looked around to see if anyone was within listening distance. The shadows of evening were stretching out, but he did not see anyone near. He said, "I'll start with something kind of close to home. There was a couple of fellows who worked for the same outfit I'm with. The Crown Butte Ranch. Their names are Paul Beckwith and George Crandall."

Not speaking very loud, she said, "I know who they are. They've been in. And I doubt that it would surprise you to know that Mr. Crandall has tried his charms."

"That doesn't surprise me. But I was wondering if you ever happened to hear anything about them dealing in loose stock—cattle, that is."

She shook her head. "No, not really."

"I didn't expect it, but it was worth a try. Here's another. Do you know a fellow named Josh Armitage?"

"Oh, yes. He's been around."

They came to the end of a block and crossed the street. Still seeing no one nearby, Elwood asked, "What's your impression of him?"

"A bit strange, actually. He comes around and says flattering things, makes as if he'd like to ask me out, but he doesn't have much spark. I don't know how to put it. It's not as if he wants to court someone and doesn't know how, but rather as if he wants to have the appearance of doing the courting. Kind of going through the motions, as if there was some other motive but I wouldn't know what. It's not as if he wanted to make off with a sack of flour or get into the cash box. But something. Like I say, it's curious."

"Sounds like it."

"By the way, this isn't anything I've seen, but I have heard that those first two men you mentioned have either gone to work for him or are in some way, um, affiliated."

"Huh. That makes sense. They got into some trouble a little while back, and I had the sense that he might have helped them get back into circulation. They were on foot in Hartville, and he showed up there with a fellow named Driggs. By the way, do you know him?"

She shook her head. "No, I don't."

"Well, back to these other two. The next time I saw them, they said they were still looking for a job, but that could be a falsehood or, as you said, they might not be actually working for him."

"It's hard to say. What I heard was hazy, and I don't ask many questions."

"Just as well." Elwood glanced around. "How about a man named Angell Gunn?"

She halted for one step and moved on. "That one."

"Do you think he has any relation to any of these others?"

"Nothing that I've seen or heard, but I've tried to have as little to do with him as possible."

"What does he buy?"

"Cartridges the first time, then one little thing at a time after that. Gun oil. Liniment. Saleratus. Whenever he buys something, he's got a comment to go along with it. And his laugh. Excuse me for saying this, but he strikes me as a very lewd man as well."

"I couldn't disagree. But moving on, did he, or anyone else, buy a roll of jute twine?"

She frowned in thought. "Not that I recall. Why?"

"I think someone's been out to get me. You remember that piece of saddle leather I bought? Well, someone cut my cinch strap, and that's why I had to replace it. Then more recently, someone set a trap along a trail I ride. Set up a shotgun with some twine across the trail so my horse would trip it."

Sylvie gave a deeper frown. "That's no small thing. If anyone should be buying cartridges, it's you."

"That's what I think."

Her dark eyes held him. "You can't let someone get away with that. You know what they'll try next, and you can't let them get away with that, either."

"Well, I don't know if it's one of these men I mentioned, and even if I did, I couldn't just walk up to him and put a hole in him for it."

A half smile played on her face. "I don't know. Some things are justified. At any rate, you can't let them get to you first."

"Thanks for the encouragement. It goes without saying that if you get wind of something, I wouldn't mind hearing it, too. If it's something you don't mind passing on."

"This is the first I've heard of these things, but I'll keep my ears open."

"I appreciate it." They came to another corner. As Elwood looked up and down the cross street, he said, "It's starting to get dark. Do you think we should be heading back toward your quarters?"

"Pretty soon. We can go one more block and then turn left." When they stepped up onto the next sidewalk, she said, "By the way, Mr. McDowell made a comment that might have had something to it."

"What was that?"

"After you left the store, he said something to the effect that Mrs. Sullivan was getting a reprieve from the visitors she had at the ranch this season. I had the feeling he was sounding me out to see what I knew, but I had nothing to offer."

Elwood thought it was only fair that he share information with Sylvie, as she had been open with him, and furthermore he sensed that it would be good for him to get some of it out.

"There is a story," he began, "and you may have heard some part of it. You know, Mrs. Sullivan had a friend from their younger days, a Mrs. Newton, who came to stay earlier in the summer."

"I think I might have heard something about that, but nothing more than what you just said."

"Well, there was an intrigue that came out of it. It's a shorter story now than if I had told it earlier, and I can give you the outline. I hope you're not too delicate."

She smiled. "Not for the outline. All stories are interesting, at least potentially."

He took a full breath. "This one might be. Anyway, Mrs. Newton came out to visit, and she let it become known, at least to me, that she had left her husband. She and I developed something of an interest, and then, from what I understood, her husband came and fetched her. This happened at about the time we went out on roundup, so I was more or less left in the dark, or standing in the rain, or however you might want to put it."

"That doesn't sound like a good way to do things."

"It wasn't, at least not for me. Then, a couple of months later, she came back. This time she said she succeeded at getting rid of her husband and needed to think about what she was going to do next."

"She told you this?"

"Yes."

"Then she got you back on the string."

"That's one way of putting it. After she was here a while, another fellow came out. They're all from Omaha, by the way. His name is Burgess, and as it turns out, he was the one who bolstered her up, as she put it, and apparently footed the bill for keeping the husband in his place."

"The husband must have been an unpleasant character in his own right."

"Quite a cad, to use her word, and maybe a little bit crooked as well."

"It sounds as if she had a good vocabulary."

Elwood laughed. "She did. And I think I even rise a level when I'm talking about it all. Anyway, the long and the short of it is that this fellow Burgess waits her out and takes her back to Omaha with him."

"And that's the end of the story?"

"As I know it, and I don't think the outcome is much of a secret."

"Mr. McDowell must have been fishing for details, then." After a second she added, "Don't worry. I won't be telling him any of this."

"I appreciate that, but the story's done, anyway."

"I hope so, for your sake. You can't let someone do things like that to you."

"It was more a matter of what she didn't do than what she did, but I know what you mean. I just have to get over it and not let it keep me from dealing with these other things I have to deal with. It had my mind clouded for a while there."

"Everything in its place," she said. "I realize this woman must have meant something to you, but like I said, you can't let someone do things like that to you, and you can't let it keep having an effect on you."

"I can't say that she did these things *to* me, but again, I agree with you. As for the effect, I suppose it'll take some time."

"You could just rub it out. But that's up to you."

He shrugged and stole a look at her. He was barely getting to know her, but he liked her spirit. "Is this our corner?" he asked.

"Yes, it is. We can turn left here."

Chapter Twelve

Elwood heard the fluting song of a meadowlark as he pulled the steel comb through the light-colored mane of the sorrel horse. He had the illusion that Josephine might come walking out of the ranch house and into the sunlight at any minute, though he knew she was gone. He could feel her absence, just as at other times he could feel the absence of Beckwith and Crandall here at the ranch.

The meadowlark sang again, the notes as clear as someone pinging on crystal. Josephine would have liked to hear it. She took interest in the trilling and chirping and warbling of the songbirds as well as the muted honking of the nighthawks in the evening and the hoot of the owl at night. As his mind wandered, he could almost hear the owl in the cold air of winter, when the sun slipped behind the buttes at four in the afternoon, painting the sky vermilion and leaving the air so thin that the owl's haunting voice sounded like a personal message.

But she hadn't stayed to hear the sounds of fall and winter, the cry of geese and the whistling of ducks as they flew over at sunset, the piercing howl of a coyote that seemed but a few feet away in the darkness. Nor would she see the sights—a deer with his antlers glinting at sunrise, a brown hawk skimming over a field of snow, an eagle picking at the carcass of a cow.

She had taken an interest in all of this, right down to the ants that crawled in and out of the yellow silk blossoms of the prickly pear, but she had been able to get up and leave it all without a look back. She had wanted a change in her life, but not a change this big. She had spirit, and she could have taken a few tough challenges, but he couldn't imagine her, over a period of time, making a little go a long way. He smiled at the thought of women he had known of who used the same water to bathe the baby, mop the floor, and water the trees at the garden's edge. And though it pained him to admit it, he was convinced she was practical enough to prefer a comfortable income, and the house that went with it, over the wages of a hired man on horseback.

A tune began to play through his head as he brushed the sorrel horse's back and sides and haunches. It was the song about the girl from Silver Springs, whose ways seemed so strange to the young cowpuncher. As Elwood recalled, the cowboy called himself "a stranger to her ways," and in the end, they were strangers to one another.

Elwood laid the blanket on the horse's back, smoothed it, and swung the saddle up and onto the blanket. That was it. Josephine and Burgess were strangers in this world, just as he was a stranger in theirs. But after all, it was his world that mattered, this part of the country where he lived by its ways. Anyone who didn't, anyone who was false or crooked, was a stranger of sorts. That might include Angell Gunn as well as Josephine and Burgess, Crandall and Beckwith. He just needed to keep track of the ones who were still around.

He pulled the latigo, buckled the rear cinch, then picked the bridle off the saddle horn and worked the bit into the horse's mouth. The tune was still going through his head as he walked the horse out and pulled the latigo another notch. He swung aboard and reined the horse around, and as he left the ranch yard at a fast walk he sang one stanza to himself.

Darlin', don't be a stranger
When time is on your hands.

You're just one range over
In a large and lonesome land.

He sang it half a dozen times, until the song of a meadowlark reminded him to keep his ears open to the world around him.

The sorrel horse snuffled as Elwood sat with both hands on the saddle horn and watched the line shack from a half mile away. With Beckwith and Crandall on the loose, Sullivan decided to send Elwood over to see if anyone had been hanging around. From this distance, everything looked uneventful. No signs of life came from the shack, and no horses were tied at the rail or standing in the corral.

A magpie flew in, landed on a corral post, and sat for a couple of minutes. Without any apparent provocation, it lifted into the air and flew away. After another minute, Elwood started down the gentle slope toward the shack.

He did not see any fresh tracks or horse droppings around the building or in the corral, so he tied up at the rail and went in.

The inside always seemed smaller than he expected. Two bunks, a table, and a small potbellied stove didn't leave much room in a twelve-by-sixteen area. The room was bare, with only the kerosene lamp on the table and a few scraps of kindling in the corner by the stove. The board surface of the table had a thin layer of dust, and a dead moth lay on the seat of one of the chairs.

Elwood sat in the other chair. He was estimating the time of day and staring at the board floor when his horse whinnied. He had left the door ajar, so he got up and went to a spot where he could look out without moving the door. He could not see anyone coming, but he thought he heard the thud of hooves on the dry ground. He opened the door, stepped partially into view, and saw a rider fifty yards away. In the first instant he recognized the upturned hat brim and gray vest of George Crandall. The horse was a common-looking brown animal that carried its head a little lower than normal, and Crandall did not seem to be carrying a rifle, a bedroll, or any other gear.

Crandall waved as he rode on in. He dismounted, tied up his horse, and flexed his arms as he stretched. "Hullo, El," he said. "Just like old times."

"Afternoon, George. What brings you over this way?"

"Just out noodlin' around." Crandall smiled, and flecks of tobacco were visible on his teeth. "How long you been here?"

Elwood had the feeling that Crandall had been following him, and there was no good reason not to tell the truth at the moment anyway, so he said, "I just got here."

"Mind if I come in and sit down for a few minutes? Rest a little."

"No, come on in. As you know, there's two chairs. If Paul shows up, one of us can sit on a bunk."

"I wouldn't expect him right away."

Elwood shrugged. "It's all the same. Cow-camp rules." He stood aside and let Crandall walk in.

Crandall took the chair nearest to the door. He tipped it up to shake off the dead moth, then rotated it so he could straddle it and sit on it backwards. He sat with his back to the door and the table to his left, and he hiked his foot onto the chair rung so that he sat tilted to one side with his gun hand draped on his thigh.

As soon as Elwood sat down, Crandall drew his .45 and rested it on his knee. The barrel was pointed straight at Elwood's mid-section.

Elwood frowned. "What's that for, George? You know that's not good manners in a cow camp, and you also know I don't like someone pointin' a gun at me."

Crandall gave his wide grin. "Then this'll be the last time I do it. As for manners, no one needs to know about it except you and me."

"Was that your shotgun?"

Crandall closed his mouth and brought his eyebrows together. "What shotgun are you talkin' about?"

"Someone planted one on the trail the other day. It went off. Almost got me."

"Don't know a thing about it."

"Whoever did it had it set up with a trip wire—actually, twine. Good flexible stuff. That's how I set it up here. Right in back of you."

Crandall's mouth opened as he turned to look over his shoulder. His gun barrel moved as well, and the distraction gave Elwood just enough time to pull his own six-gun and thumb the hammer. As Crandall brought his gun back around, Elwood pulled the trigger.

The roar of gunfire filled the cabin. Crandall slid backward off the chair and landed on the floor sitting up with his legs stretched out.

Blood seeped from his mouth as he said, "Well, that was a dirty—" He raised his gun in slow motion, and the barrel wavered.

Elwood shot him again. Crandall fell back, and his gun clunked on the floor between his legs. Everything was quiet in the shack until Elwood said, "I didn't think you had it in you to try something like that. It's too bad you did."

Elwood sat still and listened. His mouth was dry, and his heart was racing. He expected Beckwith to show up any minute, and he needed a plan. For one thing, he needed to get Crandall's body out of the way so that it wouldn't block the door. He thought about putting it on a bunk, as a decoy, but it wouldn't fool anyone for more than a minute, and hoisting the dead weight could turn into more work than he expected. He could stash it behind the door, or he could drag it outside. He didn't like having it inside, but if he dragged it out he would leave marks in the dirt and maybe blood smears in the doorway, plus he might be only halfway through the job when Beckwith showed up. He stared at the floor, not sure what to do.

He shook his head. What was he thinking? He didn't have to stay here. Not one more minute. What was done was done. This shack was as much a trap as it was a protection. It was no kind of fortress. Someone could put bullets through it or burn it down.

He saw that he still had his gun in his hand. He stood up, slid it into his holster, and rubbed his palms on his trousers. Positioning himself above the body, he pushed the door almost closed, then grabbed both wrists and pulled. Crandall's head sagged back, and Elwood had to heave with his own weight to pull the body around and settle it out of the way. He stood up and sucked in a breath. As he expected, the body had left a smear of blood on the floor. No time to waste. He bent over and picked up Crandall's six-gun and hat. Now he hesitated. He could use the extra gun, but he didn't want to have the evidence on him. He dropped the gun between the body and the wall, set the hat on the dead man's chest, and took a look around. This was as good as he could do.

He opened the door and came face to face with Paul Beckwith. His heart sank with a jolt as he saw the dark stubble, the hook nose, and the close-set eyes.

"Where's George?"

Elwood's eyes roved over the dusty black hat and gray collar until they came back to Beckwith's dark, menacing eyes. Elwood motioned backward with his head. "He's inside."

"What's he doing there?"

"He's not feelin' well. He was here when I got here."

"Let me see. Move aside." Beckwith had a firm set to his

mouth as he pushed forward.

Elwood stood back, opening the door all the way. Beckwith stepped past, settling his hand on the dark handle of his pistol. He stopped in the middle of the room.

"I don't see him."

As Beckwith pulled his gun and turned around, Elwood moved to the other side of the open doorway. Beckwith's close-set eyes showed surprise at the body on the floor, and then they were glaring, searching for a target as they swept past the bright doorway and tried to pick up Elwood. The muzzle of the .45 moved as Beckwith did. His hand tensed and his cheek winced, and the blast of the gun shook the air in the room. Elwood was sidestepping again and raising his gun as the bullet went past. He held still and squeezed the trigger.

Gunfire roared, and Beckwith staggered. His hat fell off, and his face was scrunched. His gun hung at his side. He tried to raise it with both hands, but his knees buckled. The gun clattered on the floor as Beckwith fell in a heap.

Elwood was sure he had no time to waste now. For as much as he knew, Driggs would show up next. He might even be waiting outside. Elwood took a calming breath. *Fool.* He hadn't reloaded after the gunfight with Crandall. He took the time to do it now, trying to keep his hands steady as he pushed in the cartridges.

He went to the doorway and peeked out. All three horses were still tied to the hitching rail, and the rest of the world outside looked as if nothing had disturbed the calm of a sunny afternoon. Elwood stepped outside, edged to the corner of the shack, and looked around. The corral was still empty, and a magpie sat again on one of the posts. It caught sight of Elwood and fluttered away, veering and dipping and then leveling off as it flew westward.

A faint breeze stirred as Elwood put the other two horses in the corral. After a look inside the shack to make sure nothing had moved, he closed the door. He took one more sweep of the country, mounted up, and rode off the way he had come in.

His sense of order told him to go back to the ranch first and report what had happened. He hoped Rand Sullivan would want to go with him to tell the deputy sheriff, as the line shack was property of the Crown Butte Ranch.

Elwood kept his eyes open as he rode. Twice he changed directions, moving from one familiar trail to another. By mid-afternoon he was still several miles from the ranch house. He was tired and thirsty. The scene at the line shack had taken a lot out of him, leaving him washed-out and on edge. His canteen was half full when he left there, but he had finished off most of it in the first couple of miles. Now he had about one swallow left, and he was putting it off for as long as he could.

The two horses in the corral would be getting thirsty, too. Beckwith's saddle had a rifle and a scabbard tied to it, and Elwood had been tempted for a minute to take it. But he didn't like taking something that wasn't his, especially from a dead man, and he had a rifle of his own at the bunkhouse. From now on, he would pack it along. He had the feeling that this trouble wasn't over.

Trouble. He wondered if Josephine would even understand it. To him, it was something always to be prepared for. If someone came for him, it was either him or the other man. No time to think about the rules or to match it with an idea. Maybe a man never went through it, but he was always ready. Maybe he went through it once, and the rest of his life was calm. Even at that, he had to be ready for a next time.

The idea of Josephine with the baby and the bathwater was unlikely enough, but two men with guns drawn in a line shack would have been as foreign to her as assassins in *The Arabian Nights* or cannibals in *Robinson Crusoe*. And God help her if—

Something whistled in front of him, passing with a concussion of air, and the sorrel horse lifted its front feet and twisted to the side. As Elwood pulled on the reins and dug in with his knees, he heard the booming crash of a rifle.

He fought the horse under control, turned it in a circle, and spurred it out straight into a run. The rifle boomed two more times, and the shots passed behind him. He spurred the horse again and leaned forward.

The next shot rippled in front of him, and the horse jerked to the right, throwing him forward and almost overboard. He grabbed the saddle horn with one hand and clawed to keep hold of the reins with the other. The horse kept running. Elwood lost one stirrup, and the horse was going uphill now, which caused it to rock as it reached out for more ground.

Over the top of the rise, Elwood stopped the horse and slid off. His legs felt unsteady, so he bent over and took a couple of breaths before he inspected the horse. Finding no nicks or wounds, he held onto the reins as he walked to the low crest he had just come over. He took off his hat and moved one slow step at a time until the country came into his view.

Three quarters of a mile away, across a shallow dip of grassland, sat a small hill with a crust of sandstone across the top. Motion beyond it showed a man turning a horse in a circle, trying to get on, slipping down, and trying again. After a few attempts, the man rolled up into the saddle and jerked the horse still. From the distance, Elwood thought he recognized the light-colored duster and muddy-colored horse of Angell Gunn.

The horse headed north, then northeast, in the direction of town. Elwood decided to give it a run. He would try to get close enough to Angell Gunn that the man couldn't deny what he was up to this time. He would have stuck his rifle in his scabbard, so if he decided to stop and try to make a stand, Elwood would have time to get out of range. Meanwhile, shooting a pistol from a running horse, and aiming backwards, wasn't a very good bet, and Elwood would not have to come within pistol range to make an identification.

Elwood swung aboard and put the spurs to the sorrel horse. The light-colored mane lifted in the wind and almost brushed his face as he leaned forward. The horse went down the slope, across the level area, and up the other side, eating up the ground with its stride. Within the first mile, Elwood was sure he was gaining, and he figured they had eight or nine miles to go before they reached town. He wondered if Angell Gunn could hold out that long on a hard ride, and even if the man did, he would have accusations to face. It was more likely he would try to make a stand.

The horse in the distance wasn't going any faster, and it even seemed to slow as it made its way across a broad, sparse area. Elwood hung on and kept riding.

The land began to slope upward to the north, and a mile ahead it rose into a line of hills. Elwood thought his man might try something on the other side of the ridge.

The muddy-colored horse slowed down, and the jolting steps caused Angell Gunn to bobble. He brought the horse to a complete stop, got himself settled, and took off again. In the meanwhile, Elwood closed up another quarter of a mile.

The brown horse and pale rider disappeared over the crest of the hill, and Elwood was wary of riding right over behind them. Instead, he rode east a quarter of a mile and crossed there. As he did, he saw the muddy-colored horse disappear behind a low outcropping of sandstone.

He crossed back the way he came, rode west almost half a mile, and dismounted. He walked to the crest and looked over. He found the rocks he had seen before, and although he could not locate Angell Gunn, he saw the hindquarters of the horse and the swishing tail. The bushwhacker would have his rifle out again, but if Elwood could spook the horse, he might have the man in a good spot.

It would mean leaving his own horse ground-hitched, but he felt he had the advantage, so he was willing to take the risk. He unbuckled his spurs, put them in his saddlebag, and plotted his course.

Angell Gunn would be watching the trail, so as long as the horse didn't spot Elwood first, he might be able to get within twenty yards or less. Elwood drew his gun, kept the rocks in the way so that they blocked his view of the horse and everything, and sidestepped down the slope. Time dragged, and the sun beat down.

At last he reached a point where only a low wall of sandstone stood between him and the spot where he had seen the horse. By now he had decided he would try to get the drop on Angell Gunn or to spook the horse, whichever came handiest.

With a rock in his left hand and his gun in his right, he crouched at the edge of the sandstone. He heard motion and a muttering sound, and he raised his head just high enough to see Angell Gunn leading the horse out of the nest of rocks and pointed toward town. The rifle was in the scabbard, and the man was taking labored steps.

Now was the chance. Elwood set the rock on the ground and rose up. He cocked his pistol, held it with both hands, and called out, "Stop right there!"

Angell Gunn whirled, brushed back his duster, and pulled out a pistol. With his chin raised and his lower lip pushing upward, he fired one, two, three times. Fragments of sandstone flew as Elwood ducked. When he looked around the edge of the formation, Angell Gunn had his gun in hand and was trying to get his foot in the stirrup. He gave a heave, and the horse jumped away from him. As he yanked on the rein, Elwood rose and called out.

"Hold it right there!"

Angell Gunn swung the pistol and blazed again. This time Elwood fired back, and Angell Gunn fell squat on the ground. Blood was spilling over his belly from a hole above it. He said, "You little son of a bitch, you're not worth a pot of piss." He fired again, and Elwood ducked behind the rock.

No sound came for a long moment until Elwood heard something like a body rolling over or a person trying to get up.

Elwood lowered himself to all fours and looked around the edge of the rock. Angell Gunn lay on his back with his arm outstretched and his pistol lying loose in his hand. His shirt clung to his belly and glistened with blood, but his abdomen did not move up and down. The muddy-colored horse stood a hundred yards away, cropping grass.

Elwood sat on a rock so he could catch his breath and gather his thoughts. Someone was out to get him and had been trying for a while. Angell Gunn's reappearance on his trail assured him of that. Even Crandall and Beckwith, as capable as they were of being treacherous, had not pulled a gun on him before. Today's moves, plus the spring gun a few days earlier, were way out of proportion for trying to protect the theft of a few cattle. Crandall and Beckwith had moved past that, and Angell Gunn was probably not at that level to begin with.

Elwood thought hard to try to pull things together as the afternoon shimmered around him. He figured the whole scheme flowed through Armitage, but he couldn't put his finger on why. He doubted that it had anything to do with Burgess. He got what he wanted, and he took it back with him to Omaha. He was in the past, and Elwood could scratch him from the list.

That was twice that Omaha didn't have a connection. But maybe the traveler named Stanley did. He and the man he knew about, Jim Farley, and the man who came later, Robinett.

Elwood cast another glance at the body of Angell Gunn.

Enough had happened today that he had better go to town first. He needed to report these things before someone else did, and he needed to find out anything he could about a handful of characters.

Elwood stood up. Except for the dead man, the afternoon had returned to normal. The muddy-colored horse was still grazing, and the sun, still bright, was starting to slip in the west. From somewhere not far away came the song of a meadowlark.

Chapter Thirteen

Elwood noted a look of surprise on Sylvie's face as she came into the parlor of the house where she lodged.

"El. I wondered who it could be. Mrs. Wallace said I had a visitor, but I couldn't imagine what it was. I wouldn't have expected you at this time of day, not to mention during the week."

"I had some things come up. I thought I should tell you about them, and I wanted to see if there was anything you knew about a couple of other characters." Holding his hat at his side, he glanced around the room. "Is this a good place to talk?"

She gave him a quick study, as if reading a story in the dust and stains on his clothes. "We can sit outside. I'll go for a shawl and let Mrs. Wallace know where I'll be."

She returned a few minutes later, wearing a dark-blue shawl that was a shade darker than her dress. She was wearing lipstick now as well.

Elwood put on his hat as he followed her outside. In the sky above, the last traces of evening were giving way to night. He said, "Shall we walk, or is there a place where you were planning to sit?"

"There's a seat and a couple of chairs in the backyard where we sit sometimes in the afternoon or evening. Sort of private. No one will bother us there." She led the way down the steps and around back.

In the dusk he made out two wooden chairs that looked like

old dining-room chairs. Next to them, with its back to the house, was a wooden seat wide enough for two people. It had a high back and an armrest on each end.

"We can sit here," she said.

He sat down, just a hand's width away from her, and took off his hat in the cool of the night. "Well, I had a little trouble," he said.

"I might have guessed it."

He rubbed at his trousers where he could see the bloodstain, even in the dusk. "It was in two parts. First off, I went to a line shack that belongs to the ranch, and Crandall showed up not long afterwards. He pulled a gun on me, and I had to do something about it."

"So you got the best of him."

"Yes, I did. And I was just getting my wits together when his partner, Beckwith, showed up. He didn't give me much choice, either. Not that I expected him to, with his partner lyin' on the floor behind the door."

"So they're both done for."

"It was either them or me. I don't think I would have been so lucky if they hadn't been so sure of themselves."

"But they came after you?"

"Oh, yeah. No question about it. Things changed when they went to work for what's-his-name. That is, I assume they were working for him. They were riding horses that had the same brand as the ones Armitage and Driggs were riding. You say you don't know Driggs."

"No."

"Well, I saw him with Armitage a couple of times. Out on work."

"Some kind of work," she said, "if those other two came after you."

"I just count myself lucky. I'm no gun hand, but a man's got to know how to take care of himself if trouble comes calling."

"And it came twice."

He widened his eyes just at the memory. "Twice there, and again later in the day. When I was on my way back to the ranch, someone took some shots at me."

"Did you get to see who it was?"

"Oh, yes. It was your friend and mine, Angell Gunn. After he missed a few times, he lit out for town. I took off after him. I wanted to get close enough so that he couldn't deny I saw him. But the going got rough for him, and he holed up. I was able to sneak up on him, and then he opened up on me with his pistol, so—well, he ended up like the other two."

"Whew! You mean he's done for, too."

"That's right."

"I'd say good riddance, but that's probably not the end of things."

"I don't think so. His horse didn't have a brand on it, but I'd guess he was working for the same outfit. I just don't know why, and that's what I need to work on. Meanwhile, I loaded him up and took him into town. That's how I got the blood on my pants. When I got here, I found out the deputy is gone for two days. So I left him, the body, at the barbershop and came to see you."

"What do you plan to do next?"

"I don't know yet. I'm still trying to catch my breath." He turned to her, and he could see her features in the thickening dusk. "I don't know what's behind all of this, but you might be able to help me find out."

"I'll tell you what I can."

He didn't know if there was a note of reservation in her voice, and he didn't know if telling what she could was the same as telling what she knew, but he went ahead. "I imagine you heard about a traveler who came through town here, a fellow named

Stanley. They found him dead in the livery stable."

"I remember that story. I didn't meet him, though."

"He stayed overnight at the ranch, and we saw him again here in town. He had a drink with us. Friendly sort. While we were in the saloon, there was another fellow, all dressed up like he ran a gambling hall. He was sounding off, buying drinks, telling everyone his name was Jim Farley. The Irishman."

She moved her arm closer to her body.

"Then Mr. Stanley, just off the cuff, told us the man's name wasn't Jim Farley at all. He said his name was Jude Ostrander, and he was a bank robber who pulled a big job in Topeka." Elwood waited for Sylvie to say something in response.

"He was right." Her shawl went up and down as she took a breath. "Like I said, I didn't know Mr. Stanley, but I know Jude Ostrander. He's a bank robber, all right, and he'd sell his own mother. He pulled a big job in Topeka, a big job, and he left everyone else holding the bag. Two of them were killed, one went to jail, and the other three have been looking for him."

"Stanley said Jude was the only one who knew where the money was."

"That's Jude. And that's why he's been on the dodge. Naturally, he'd like to go back and get it all. For himself. And even if he did let the others in at this point, they might want to do away with him once they got it."

"He said he was on his way to Idaho."

"Like I'm on my way to Paris."

Elwood thought she had all the bitterness of an ex-lover, but he didn't want to know something like that at the moment, and he didn't want to get off the trail he was on. So he said, "Did he talk to you when he came through town?"

"He looked me up. That's why he came this way." Then with a note of humor she added, "On his way to Idaho."

"So it must have been a matter of chance that he and Stanley crossed paths."

"I would guess so. I never heard of Stanley before I came here. To tell you the truth, I didn't know any of the other members except for Jude and my brother Jemy."

"Your brother?"

"Yes. He's the one who ended up in jail. And sweet, mealymouthed Jude came by to see if there was anything I knew that he didn't. I wouldn't have told him if I did, but I didn't know a thing, so it was easy to tell him that."

"I'm sorry to hear of your brother getting mixed up with that kind of a bunch."

"So am I, but he chose that way, and he should get out in a few years."

Elwood thought back. "You say you didn't know any of the others. What do you think of the possibility that this fellow Armitage might be one of them, or working for one of them?"

"I don't know. It's possible. He's got the character for it."

"How about a man named Jennings? Armitage works for him, running his ranch. Says Jennings is from Pennsylvania, but at this point you've got to wonder. But it's obvious he's not from here."

"I don't recognize the name, but like I said, I didn't know any of the others."

"One more. There was a man named Robinett came through, not long ago, asking about Stanley. He might well have been looking for Jim Farley—or Jude Ostrander, that is."

"I don't know him, either."

"Maybe he came by the store. Medium build, light-blue suit and hat."

Sylvie shook her head. "Doesn't sound familiar at all."

"Always worth a try." Elwood took a long breath. "Well, I guess that's as much as I had in mind for right now."

"I wish I knew more. But I've told you everything I know."

"I appreciate it." He stood up with his hat in his hands.

She stood up and faced him, her features dark and shadowy and appealing. "Are you going back now?"

He made himself stick to business. "To the ranch? I think I'd better. There's not anything else I can do at the moment, and I need to see what the boss says."

"Take care, El."

"I will. You do the same."

Her eyes met his in the moonlight. "I'm all right. You're the one I worry about."

"Thanks. But let's not worry any more than we have to." He touched her cheek, then put on his hat and walked her to the door.

Elwood set out for the line shack as the sun was coming up. Rand Sullivan said he would go into town and see if he could get the deputy to ride with him sooner.

The palomino was fresh and moved out at a trot. Elwood was tired after the long day he had put in the day before, but he wanted to get to the line shack before anyone else did. The boss had agreed that for the time being Elwood could take the horses to water and put them back in the corral. If they got a deputy out there, they could load the bodies onto the two horses and take them back to town. If not, they might have to do it themselves. They could decide when the time came.

Elwood drew rein on the palomino at his usual spot a half mile from the shack. Things had changed. Only one horse stood in the corral, and it was lighter in color than either of the two he had left in the corral the day before. A cleft of darkness showed where the door of the shack was open.

He guessed that either Driggs or Haden was holed up inside and had already seen him. That put a kink in things. Still, he needed to know for sure who was there. He turned the palomino and rode back down the slope out of sight from the shack.

The best way to approach it, he decided, was from the back. The little building had only one window on the corral side, and with the position of the door, the back side would be the blindest. The palomino still had plenty of pep, so Elwood let the horse lope on a wide half circle to the north. Again he came up to a vantage point about a half mile out, and this time he could see the west side of the shack, which lay in shadow. As Elwood narrowed his eyes, he thought he saw a form in the shade.

Dismounting, he took his binoculars from the saddlebag and focused in. Sure enough, there was a man sitting up against the building. His hat lay in his lap, and his head leaned back to touch the wall.

Elwood lowered the binoculars, then raised them to take another look. The man had a brown beard and thick brown hair. He lolled his head to one side and the other, but he did not seem to be on the lookout. Elwood took him to be Haden, and he guessed that the man was either drunk or wounded.

Back out of sight with the horse, Elwood took off his spurs and put them away. He walked about thirty yards to the left and came up for another look. The shack sat at an angle, and Elwood could see neither the front door nor the shady side. As long as the man didn't move, Elwood would be out of sight as well.

He hung onto the reins in case he needed a fast getaway, and keeping a steady eye on the building, he walked down the slope toward it. Part of the corral was in sight, but the horse wasn't. When he reached the corner of the shack, even the corral was shut out.

Elwood took a deep breath as he drew his gun. Still leading the horse, he took slow, careful steps to the next corner. He set his hat on the saddle horn and edged his way until he could see into the shade next to the building. The man hadn't moved, and he did not have a gun in his hand. He did have one in his holster, so there was a good chance he didn't have one hidden in his lap beneath his hat.

Elwood stepped around the corner with his gun still drawn. "Are you Haden?" he asked.

The man opened his eyes and stared but did not answer. His face was pale.

"I said, is your name Haden?"

"Yeah. Gus Haden." He gritted his teeth and clenched his teeth, and his face colored a little.

Elwood noticed a red stain, some of it dry and some of it moist, on Haden's shirt above his belt. "It looks like you've been shot."

"Do you have any water?"

Elwood turned to the palomino, took his hat from the saddle horn, and put it on. He led the horse to the corral and tied it, then unwrapped the canteen strap from the saddle horn. He kept an eye on Haden all the time, but Haden's eyes were closed. Elwood carried the water back to the shade. He said, "Here" as he knelt by the man's side and handed him the canteen.

Haden opened his eyes. "Thanks." He unscrewed the cap and drank about a quart from the half-gallon canteen. "Thanks," he said again as he handed it back. "You're the one that got us fired, aren't you?"

"Not really, but it doesn't matter. Where's your pal Driggs?"

Haden took a deep breath and sat motionless for a minute with his tongue between his lips. "I needed that water," he said.

"Well, there's more."

Haden raised his chin and scratched his neck. "Mac's dead," he said.

"That's too bad. How did it happen?"

"The crooked sons a bitches did it."

"Armitage and who else?"

"Armitage did it, but Jennings was there."

"I thought Jennings was in Pennsylvania."

Haden made a spitting sound. "Ah, he never went anywhere. He's been here all this time."

"So how did it happen?"

Haden closed his eyes, and Elwood thought he was going to have to prompt him again, but then Haden opened his eyes and spoke. "First, they sent us over here. Me an' Mac. We found your two friends, dead. I guess you knew about that. We took 'em back and buried 'em."

"To the Drumm?"

"No, they moved camp. They're at the other place, south of here."

"The place that used to be Norville's?"

"That's it."

"So why did Armitage shoot you after you did all that work?"

Haden shook his head. "Stupidest damn thing. All this time, they're tryin' to get someone to go back to Iowa and kidnap the Ostrander kid."

"Really? What for?"

"To get him to talk."

"Ostrander? They've got the fella who said he was Jim Farley? Have they had him all this time?"

"Oh, yeah. That's why they moved. They thought someone was gettin' close."

"So they wanted someone to kidnap his son?"

Haden's chest went up and down as he took a breath. "Yeah. First they wanted us to do it, and we said no. Then they hired these other two and tried to get them to do it, and they stalled. So when they got killed, it was back to me an' Mac. We said we didn't want to, so Armitage decided to get tough, and we had it out right there. They killed Mac, but they had too much on their hands to follow me. I expect 'em sooner or later, though." Haden licked his lips and swallowed.

"That's too bad. Seems to me they get away with way too much."

Haden's voice was raspy. "Oh, hell. You don't know half of it."

"So they've got Ostrander. I suppose they're trying to get him to squawk about where the money is. And they don't want anyone to know they've got him."

"Uh-huh. That's the deal."

"So they did away with Stanley, hanged him, because he knew who Farley was and they didn't want anyone to get anything out of him."

"That was before we went to work for 'em, but that's what I understand. The poor son of a bitch."

"And they think I know, too."

"They've got you marked."

"Just for knowing Stanley."

Haden had a dull expression in his eyes as he stared at Elwood. "They think someone's lookin' to spring Ostrander, and they think you might be a helper."

"Who would want to spring him? Not someone from the gang. They've already got him."

Haden put his tongue between his lips and breathed in through his nose. His face looked paler than before. "I'll tell you, that water made me feel better for a couple of minutes, but I'm startin' to get dizzy."

Elwood, still kneeling, held up the canteen. "There's more right here. But tell me, who wants to spring him?"

"Oh, someone who wants a cut of the loot. Didn't have the guts to do the job itself, but they think that if they can get him free, he'll owe 'em."

"If he pays."

"Huh. They've got one of 'em already. Got 'im in the same cage as Ostrander. That's what Armitage calls him. Birdie in the cage."

Elwood drew his brows together. "Do you mean a fellow named Robinett? Wears a light-blue suit, like he came from the city?"

"That's him. Angell Gunn brought him in."

"Angell Gunn. I thought he was in cahoots with the rest of 'em."

"Oh, he is. And you'd better watch out for him."

"Not anymore. He came to the end of his trail yesterday."

Haden smiled. "By God. At least one good thing happened." He pressed his lips together and swallowed hard. "How about some more of that water?"

"Oh, sure. Here it is." Elwood handed him the canteen.

Haden drank and drank, tipping the canteen up. When he lowered it he said, "Thanks. There's a little left." He opened his eyes wide and took a deep breath.

Elwood brought him back to the topic. "So do they think someone is still going to try to get Ostrander loose?"

"I think so. They've had him quite a while and he hasn't talked. I think they're afraid they're runnin' out of time."

"And they think I might help? That's daffy."

"They've got their notions, and they give the orders."

Elwood thought back for a couple of seconds. "Who set the spring gun?"

"The what?"

"The shotgun with the trip wire."

"Oh, that was Angell Gunn. He was keeping an eye on you."

"I knew that."

"And when he saw you talkin' to the new birdie, they had him try that. When it didn't work, he said he'd do things his way."

"Well, that didn't work, either."

"Too bad for him." Haden licked his lips. "I no sooner take a drink than I'm thirsty again. I should have told you, there's a canteen on my horse."

"That's all right. Take this. I'll get it in a couple of minutes."

Haden drank the last of Elwood's water. "Thanks," he said.

Elwood took the canteen and settled back on his heels. "Thanks to you for tellin' me what you have. I would have given you the water anyway, but I appreciate you talkin' to me."

"I hope they rot. Sons a bitches turn on the men that help 'em. Here I am with lead in my guts, and I'll probably die before I get to take one of 'em with me."

"Just hang on. I think you might make it."

"Don't kid me, pal. But it's good of you to stay here with me. You don't owe me anything."

"It doesn't matter now." Elwood stood up and looked around at the country. "Do you think they'll come by this way? You say they've got their hands full."

Haden's face, which had been pale all along, seemed to have a tinge of blue. He moved his tongue across his lips, opened his mouth, and had to try again. "They were gonna go to town. What would you think of bringin' that other water?"

"I can do that." Elwood went to the corral, looked on both sides of the saddled horse, and saw no canteen. He went back to see Haden. "I didn't find any water. Are you sure you had some?"

"I thought I did."

Elwood glanced around. "Did you go inside once you got here?"

"I don't think so."

Elwood remembered that the door of the shack was open. "Let me see," he said. He went around front and stepped inside. The place gave him a shiver, but he didn't see any small objects except the kerosene lantern. He looked the room over a second time, trying to ignore the bloodstains on the floor, and he closed the door behind him when he went out.

Haden had his eyes closed and was breathing through his open mouth.

"I can't find it," said Elwood. "The canteen. You might not have had one."

"Maybe not."

Elwood scanned the country again. "You said they were going to town."

"Uh-huh."

"Do you know what for?"

"Huh?"

"Do you know why they were going to town?"

"Oh. To get the girl."

"What girl was that?"

"The Indian girl." Haden's voice sounded sleepy.

Elwood looked down at Haden. The man's eyes were closed. In a minute he would want more water, and there wasn't any. After the talk about the other canteen, Elwood wondered how much Haden was babbling.

Elwood frowned. "What Indian girl?"

Haden didn't move or speak.

The answer came to Elwood all in a second as he recalled the features he had seen in the dusk the night before. Of course. Lamarre. Montana. Probably trapper French, a couple of generations back. He pictured her as he had seen her in better light, with her dark hair, tan skin, and smooth complexion.

"My God. What would they want with her?"

Haden still didn't move, and Elwood knew he had gotten his last answer from the man. But he didn't need to be told. As he picked up his canteen, he said the answer out loud. He knew he was using the wrong words, but they came right out. "Jim Farley."

Chapter Fourteen

Elwood gave the strap of the canteen two wraps around the saddle horn and went back to stand in the shade for a minute. In the short time he had been at the line shack, the morning shade had receded, and the toes of Haden's boots now stuck out in the sunlight. Before long, the body would be in full sun. Yesterday's magpie would return, maybe with friends. A man deserved better than that.

Setting Haden's hat out of the way for the moment, Elwood grabbed the body by the armpits and started dragging. He got a better hold, lifted, and dragged some more, making it around the corner and to the doorway before he stopped for a breath. He opened the door and got set. With a heave he pulled the body up and over the threshold and into the room. One of Haden's spurs caught on the sill, and Elwood stumbled. Regrouping, he gave the body a turn and another pull. As he did, an object slipped out of Haden's pocket and clattered on the floor. It looked like a small pistol.

Elwood dragged the body past the open door and laid it out flat. He placed the dead man's hands on his chest and stood back. He said, "I'm sorry for you, pal."

Turning, he saw the dark pistol shining in the sunlight of the open doorway. He stooped and picked it up. It was a short-barreled, small-handled Smith and Wesson .38, and as he clicked the cylinder he saw five rounds. Elwood decided he would keep this one. He put it in his trousers pocket and went to fetch Haden's hat. He left the hat on the table.

When he stepped outside again, he searched the landscape. Nothing seemed to change out there, but according to Haden, Armitage and Jennings had been on the move. If they were going to town, they had probably been there already. If they had gotten what they went after, and if Elwood went to town, they would be way ahead of him. Plus he would have to confer with Rand Sullivan. Chances were that Armitage and Jennings were on their way to the Norville place. Elwood swept the country again. Finding them out there was a questionable proposition, but he might be able to get to Norville's ahead of them, and if not, he could get there before they had a chance to do much.

He felt a twinge of guilt for not doing what the boss expected, but Rand Sullivan knew that things could take various turns out here. Elwood went around the corner of the shack and walked toward the palomino. He spoke to the horse as he dug in the saddlebag. After putting on his spurs, he scanned the country one more time. Still nothing. The only things that seemed to change were here at the line shack—the number of horses and the number of dead men. He untied the palomino, checked his rigging, and took off.

The palomino had worked up a sweat when Elwood rode into the ranch yard. He tied up at the bunkhouse and went in.

Otis looked up from cutting meat. "What's new?"

"A little more of the same. You remember Driggs and Haden? Well, I found Haden dying at the line shack. He and Driggs had it out with their bosses. Driggs got killed, and Haden got shot up. The rest of 'em are at Norville's, and I'm going there."

"Where's Rand?"

"I imagine he's still in town. When he comes in, if I'm not back already, you can tell him where I went."

Otis twisted his mouth. "Don't you think you should wait for him?"

"They're holdin' a couple of people, tryin' to get information out of 'em, and I don't know what they might do." Elwood went to his bunk and pulled out a duffel bag from underneath.

"What kind of people?"

"From what Haden said, at least Jim Farley and that fellow Robinett." Elwood set the bag on his bunk and opened it.

"Now there's a pair."

Elwood took out the blue shirt he had worn only once. He stood up. "I guess Robinett was hopin' to spring Farley loose."

"I wouldn't put myself in too much danger for either of them." Otis stared at the shirt.

"Neither would I." Elwood motioned with the shirt. "I might need it."

Outside, he led the palomino to the hitching rail in front of the barn. He folded the .38 inside the shirt and stuffed the bundle in the saddlebag. After that he made short work of changing horses as he transferred his saddle and bridle to the dark horse. As he rode away he waved to Otis, who stood at the bunkhouse doorway wearing his white apron and smoking a thin cigarette.

Halfway to Norville's, Elwood spotted two riders in the distance. He rode the dark horse to cover behind a low hill and dismounted. He dug into the saddlebag beneath the shirt, took out the binoculars, and got a look at the two men on horseback. They were over a mile away, riding from the west. Elwood was able to identify Armitage in his black outfit, and the other man had the size and shape as well as the light-colored hat of Jennings.

Elwood frowned. He wondered what the two men would be doing out that way, and the best answer he could think of was that they were looking for Haden. They might have been to town already, or they might not have gone yet. Either way, they were headed toward the Norville place and not moving very fast. Elwood figured he could get there five or ten minutes ahead of them.

The sun was straight up and the smell of a warm horse hung in the air as Elwood held the reins in back of him and studied the Norville ranch yard. No horses were tied in front, but he counted three in the corral. Two of them looked like the ones Beckwith and Crandall had been riding, and he figured the other one might have been used by Driggs. In any case, it looked as if he had gotten in ahead of Armitage and Jennings, and he had no time to lose.

He trotted the dark horse down the slope and tied up in front of the house. His stomach was in knots, and he tried to keep his hands from shaking as he took the bundled shirt out of the saddlebag. This was it, he thought. If he didn't act nervous, he wasn't nervous.

He went to the door and knocked, and after a minute it opened. The interior of the house was dim in comparison with the bright sunlight, but he recognized Sylvie in the doorway.

Her face was expressionless as she said, "It's you."

He stepped forward and said, "I came for you. Here's a jacket. Keep you from getting sunburned." He handed her the bundle, and she stepped aside he walked in.

Two men stood toward the back of the room, both watching him. He wondered which of them was holding court, and he couldn't tell. Then the door closed behind him, and he heard a pistol click, followed by a voice he did not recognize.

"Turn around slow, and keep your hands up."

As he did so, he had to blink a couple of times. His eyes were adjusting to the dimmer light, and he was trying to make sense of the man with the gun. He wore a billed cap, and his head leaned forward.

The duck. Of course. It was just like Rand Sullivan said. There was always one more son of a bitch than you counted on.

The duck spoke again. "Hand me your gun. Then sit on the floor, take off your boots, and set your hat next to them. That's right." He took Elwood's six-shooter and stuck it in his waistband, all the time keeping his .45 pointed straight. With the hammer back, it looked ready to go off.

Elwood sat on the floor and did as he was told. He shook out each boot for good measure. When he was done he looked up at the duck and said, "Haden had a lot to say."

"Everyone does. You can stand up now." The duck moved his gun in the direction of the other two men. "You two, stay put until I say different."

Elwood stood up and began to tuck in his shirt. As he moved his hand toward the back of his waist, Sylvie passed behind him. He felt the cool metal of the gun pressed into his hand, and he moved back half a step as he held the small gun with his thumb and adjusted his palm on the handle.

The duck waved his .45 again. "Get out of the way, sister. Don't crowd anyone. Let's see that jacket."

Sylvie stood apart, held the shirt with both hands, and let it unfold downwards.

The duck's eyes followed the movement, then came back as Elwood's hand came out with the .38. Elwood fired and hit him in the chest. The duck turned with the impact as he raised his gun and jerked the trigger. A blast of air hit Elwood in the face, and the bullet tore through the door. The duck's legs went out from under him, and his .45 spilled on the floor.

Keeping an eye on the man and keeping the .38 pointed, Elwood leaned over and picked up the loose gun. When he was sure the man wasn't going to move, he leaned again and pulled his own gun from the dead man's waist. He put it in his holster.

He stood up and took a deep breath. Holding the .38 in one hand and the duck's .45 in the other, he turned to look at the two men who were watching him. One was Robinett, without his hat and jacket and looking as if he hadn't had a bath or a shave for a while. The other man was not familiar to begin with. His hair was shaggy, he had a beard, and he wore a common work shirt. But Elwood was expecting him, and within a few seconds he recognized the blue eyes and pale complexion of the man who called himself Jim Farley.

Elwood turned to Sylvie. "Is this Jude Ostrander?"

"That's him," she said.

Ostrander's voice came out in a commanding tone. "It's about time someone came for me. I've been in this pigsty and another one like it for months."

Elwood gave him a calm look and said, "I didn't come for you."

Ostrander shook his head. "Then you're not worth a damn to anyone."

"I could be, but you can decide for yourself whether you want to be agreeable or weep on acting superior."

"You'd better give us two of those guns."

"Not yet." Elwood went to the door, looked out, then closed it and turned the latch. Walking back to the middle of the room, he waved his hand at the dead body and spoke to Robinett. "This man's bosses are going to be here in a few minutes. What's his name, anyway?"

"Gleason."

"Haven't heard of him, but no matter. We've got a few minutes, and I need to know a couple of things. It might make a difference in how we get out of this."

"Let's get started." Robinett gave a quick nod as if to say he was all business.

"All right. To begin with, why were you looking for Stanley or for information about him?"

Robinett's chin shifted as his mouth tightened. "Just to find Ostrander."

"What did Stanley have to do with any of this?"

"Nothing, really."

"Then why was he even here?"

Robinett set his mouth in a firm expression again and breathed through his nose. "Burgess sent him here."

"Burgess?" So Omaha figured into it after all.

"Yeah. Somewhere along the way, Burgess met Stanley and found out about his walking expedition. He paid him a little to go by way of the Crown Butte to see if Mrs. Newton was doing what she said she was."

"Which was staying at the ranch."

"Correct."

Elwood frowned. "So he just happened to see Ostrander here and passed a remark?"

"Apparently so."

"I didn't know a thing about it," said Ostrander.

Elwood returned his attention to Robinett. "And they did him in for that?"

"They already had Ostrander, and they didn't want anyone being led to him."

"Did Armitage know Stanley was working for Burgess?"

Robinett shook his head. "Nah."

"I saw them talking together, the same night I met you."

Robinett laughed. "Burgess kept his cards close to his chest on everything."

"Then how do you know so much?"

"It's my business to know things. It's not as if I'm some sheepherder just come off the mountain."

Ostrander's voice came back in a sarcastic tone. "That's why they haven't done away with him. They think he knows something about where something is."

Robinett moved his chin forward and put his finger inside his collar, as if he was loosening the necktie that was no longer there. "Maybe I do."

Elwood moistened his lips. "That's probably enough for right now." He stepped to his left and handed the .38 to Sylvie. "Here, keep this out of sight unless we need it."

"Give me the other one," said Ostrander.

Elwood had a good memory of what Sylvie had said about Ostrander, how he would sell his own mother and had left his partners holding the bag. Elwood moved his eyes from Ostrander to Robinett. "Do you know how to use one of these?"

"Oh, yeah." Robinett took a step forward.

Ostrander moved with him. "Damn it, give me one."

"Get back," said Elwood. "Here." He handed the duck's .45 to Robinett. Keeping an eye on Ostrander, he stooped to put on his boots and then his hat. He was just standing up when the doorknob rattled.

Everyone turned. The doorknob rattled again, and a loud knocking sounded on the panel.

Elwood drew his gun and moved to the door. He recognized Jennings's voice, loud and forceful. "Open up, damn it! Open the door!"

Elwood turned the latch, stepped aside, and swung the door open. Jennings took a step forward and looked into the barrel of Elwood's gun. He had his own pistol drawn, but he lowered it.

"Give me that six-gun," said Elwood, "and be careful."

"Where's Gleason?" Jennings's gaze went downward and rested on the dead man.

"Give me the gun."

A voice came from the back of the room. "Nobody move."

Elwood kept his gun trained on Jennings as everyone turned

to see Armitage with his arm around Ostrander's throat and an ivory-handled .45 pointed against the man's temple.

"The fat's in the fire," said Armitage. "You two put your guns on the floor, or I'll pull the trigger and nobody'll ever get anything."

Elwood realized Armitage still assumed he had an interest in freeing Ostrander. With his gun still on Jennings, Elwood stepped back a pace and said, "He doesn't mean anything to me. I can shoot your boss as quick as you can do anything."

Jennings looked queasy in his cream-colored hat, brown coat, white shirt, and spreading tan vest. His face quivered, and he said, "Put down your gun, Josh. Let him go for the time being."

"Not yet. We've got control. Birdie, put your gun on the floor. Slow and easy."

Robinett stood still as his eyes moved from Armitage to Elwood.

The whinny of a horse came through the open door.

"Someone's coming," said Elwood.

Armitage barked, "Damn it, drop your gun."

"Your boss isn't doing anything," said Elwood. "We've got you two to one."

"How?" Armitage turned his eyes to Robinett, whose hands were shaking as he tried to cock the .45. "Well, by God, take this!" Armitage pulled the trigger, and blood sprayed from the other side of Ostrander's head.

Elwood swiveled as Ostrander dropped to the floor and Armitage lowered his aim. Elwood squeezed the trigger, and the roar of the gun filled the room. Armitage's black hat tumbled away as he fell against the wall and dropped.

Elwood came back around to Jennings, whose pistol was pointed down and shaking as his mouth quavered. "Not me, not me!" he pleaded.

Elwood relaxed his gun and stepped back.

Sylvie's voice startled him from behind. "Look out!"

Too late, he turned to see Robinett with both hands holding the .45 and aiming at Jennings. The gun roared, and a red spot flared on Jennings's white shirt. The man fell backward and slumped on the floor.

Elwood brought his gun halfway up as he cast a narrow look at Robinett. "You didn't have to do that."

Robinett's mustache twitched. "They killed him."

"That was already done."

"They killed him. Now nobody gets anything."

So it was true. Ostrander was the only one who knew. He was like the goose and the golden eggs.

"You ruined the whole thing," said Robinett. "You should have given him a gun."

"It didn't seem like a good idea at the time, but as it turned out, maybe I made a mistake. If I made another, it was giving you one. Once you got started, you didn't know how to stop."

"Your mistake was not letting us both have guns. Now look what it cost."

Elwood tried to hold his temper. "If you were that good, why didn't you just take Gleason's gun earlier?"

Robinett didn't answer. He stood with the gun dangling at his side as he looked past Elwood to the open door. "I thought you said someone was coming."

"I just said that because of the horse. He's a noisy one. I didn't know if anyone would believe it, but I thought it might raise the stakes." Elwood put his gun in his holster.

Robinett's voice rose as he said, "The stakes? I'll tell you, there was one hell of a lot of money at stake here."

Elwood rested the heel of his hand on the butt of his pistol as he leveled his gaze at Robinett. "And it was worth everything that everyone went through, wasn't it?"

"Then what in the hell did you come out here for?"

Elwood could hardly believe it. Here was the last of the scoundrels standing, and he still thought Elwood had an interest in the money. It was the way selfish people thought. Elwood's eyes met Sylvie's, and they both smiled. Then he answered the question.

"The only one I met who's been straight in this whole mess. Everyone else has been a stranger in one way or another."

He held his hand toward her, and together they walked out into the sunlight.

ABOUT THE AUTHOR

John D. Nesbitt lives in the plains country of Wyoming, where he teaches English and Spanish at Eastern Wyoming College. He writes western, contemporary, mystery, and retro/noir fiction as well as nonfiction and poetry. John has won many awards for his work, including two awards from the Wyoming State Historical Society (for fiction), two awards from Wyoming Writers for encouragement of other writers and service to the organization, two Wyoming Arts Council literary fellowships (one for fiction, one for nonfiction), and three Spur awards from Western Writers of America. His most recent books are *Thorns on the Rose,* a collection of western poetry, and *Dark Prairie,* a frontier mystery.